Keiko never drea...
promise her hand t...

"What kind of contract?" Kenji wanted to know, glaring at Shoji. The inscrutable look never wavered.

Her father cleared his throat again. "Ibaragi-san was a good friend. We knew each other in Japan. We went to school together, until. . .until he went to the mission school."

Kenji began to fidget, wondering where this was leading. "What kind of contract?" he asked again.

"A marriage contract between his first son and my first daughter, or my first son and his first daughter, whichever came first."

Kenji was on his feet in an instant. "Are you outta your mind? You must be if you think I'm marrying a girl I've never even met!" He shoved his hand through his slicked-back hair. "I can't believe even *you* would do such a thing!"

Keiko's eyes were on Shoji. He looked her way and for an instant his poise melted. His eyes were almost pleading. Only a moment, then the closed look returned to his face.

"He doesn't mean you, do you?" she asked her father quietly. "Mr. Ibaragi has come for me, haven't you?"

DARLENE MINDRUP is a full-time homemaker and home schoolteacher. A "radical feminist" turned "radical Christian," Darlene lives in Arizona with her husband and two children. She believes "romance is for everyone, not just the young and beautiful."

Books by Darlene Mindrup

HEARTSONG PRESENTS
HP207—The Eagle and the Lamb
HP224—Edge of Destiny

The Rising Sun

Darlene Mindrup

Heartsong Presents

To Michelle Finklea, my most avid fan (besides my husband and mom).

And to those Japanese Americans who loved this country enough to stand by it even when it didn't stand by them.

A note from the Author:
I love to hear from my readers! You may write to me at the following address: **Darlene Mindrup**
Author Relations
P.O. Box 719
Uhrichsville, OH 44683

ISBN 1-57748-195-X

THE RISING SUN

Cover illustration by Gary Maria.

one

March 1941

Keiko lifted the last item from the depths of the huge box, gently unwrapping the tissue paper from around it. She smiled at the Japanese daruma, its one colored eye giving it a somewhat strange appearance.

Lifting the doll to place it on the shelf among the others of her collection, she was careful to select a place of prominence. Settling back on her heels, she stroked her hands down her silk kimono, studying each doll's position.

Although Keiko considered herself a rather traditional American, she still loved to celebrate many of the Japanese holidays. *Hinamatsuri,* or the Doll's Festival, was her favorite.

She stared at the Bodhidharma doll. It had no arms, no legs, and only one eye. Reaching up, she gently pushed the doll over, watching as it returned to its upright position. Her thoughts went back to the day her mother had told her of its meaning.

"Mama-san, why does this doll have no legs or arms? And why is only one eye painted?" Six-year-old Keiko frowned up at her mother, her brown almond eyes filled with curiosity.

Her mother reached up, gently stroking the frown from her face. "Don't frown so, Keiko-chan. It will give you wrinkles." Lifting the little girl onto her lap, Keiko's mother's voice took on the singsong quality she used when telling a story.

"Long ago a man, Bodhidharma was his name, traveled to China. He wanted to see the great Buddha. He waited and waited, sitting in the Zen posture that Buddha likes to sit in. He waited so long that eventually he lost his arms and legs."

Keiko stared up at her mother, her mouth open. "Is this true?"

Her mother's brown eyes twinkled back at her. Hugging her close, her mother whispered in her ear. "No, my little Keiko-chan. It is just a story. But the doll is cute, do you not think so?"

Keiko's eyes went back to the doll. She tried hard not to frown, but it was a losing battle. "But it only has one eye. It looks. . .it looks. . ." She frowned again, unable to explain how the doll made her feel.

"When a girl receives a Bodhidharma doll," her mother explained, "she makes a wish, so to speak, and colors in one eye. When her wish is fulfilled, or her endeavor is completed, she colors in the other eye."

Little Keiko took the doll into her hand, stroking one finger softly over the painted eye. Glancing back up at her mother, her eyes asked the question her lips refused to utter.

"That colored eye represents you and Kenji," her mother told her quietly. "I prayed for children, and God has blessed me with two fine, beautiful angels."

Keiko looked back at the doll, her forehead puckering. "But there are two eyes and two of us."

Her mother smiled, hugging her close again. "Yes, Keiko-chan. But my one wish was for children who would come to love and serve Jesus. When that happens, then I will color in the other eye."

That had been almost twelve years ago. Keiko's eyes filled with sadness that her mother had not realized the fulfillment of her wish. Although Keiko knew and loved the Lord, her mother died before Keiko accepted Jesus as her savior.

The back screen door slammed and Keiko frowned. Without turning around she knew who was behind her. It was always the same. Kenji, so alive with energy, so volatile in his emotions.

"Hey, Sis." He stopped dead, his eyes going over her from the top of her head with its Japanese-style bun to the cork geta on her feet. His eyes darkened with anger, but he refrained from comment. Kenji hated anything that even remotely resembled Japan or Japanese ways. He considered himself only an American and wished to be treated as such, whereas Keiko was proud of her Japanese heritage.

Kenji took in the assortment of dolls lined on the shelves around the living room. Suddenly, his eyes softened. Walking over, he took a doll gently into his hands, studying it intently. Keiko saw the sheen in his eyes.

"Remember when she bought this one?" His voice was husky with suppressed tears.

Keiko nodded. "When we took our first plane trip to Oregon to visit Oba-san." Their aunt had smiled tolerantly while Mother had purchased the small doll at the airport. Mama-san had always tried to purchase dolls for her collection that would hold memories for her in the years to come.

Kenji set the doll back on the shelf and turned away. "I have baseball practice today, so I'll be late. Jason invited me for supper."

Jason and Kenji had become close friends since attending the university together. But Papa-san was not happy with their relationship. He blamed Jason for much of Kenji's anti-Japanese feelings.

Keiko bit her lip. Papa-san would not be pleased, but it would do no good to remind Kenji of this. Keiko's heart thumped hard. She should say something, but she knew from past experience it would only make Kenji angry, and then he might not come home for days.

Kenji slammed back out the door, and Keiko's eyes went back to the Bodhidharma doll. No, it looked like her mother's wish would never be fulfilled and the poor little doll would forever remain without one eye. Keiko felt the tears gathering in her throat. Where had it all gone wrong? Had it started with her mother's death six years ago? Everything seemed to have changed after that.

It amazed Keiko that her mother's strong Christian beliefs had had so little impact on her father and brother. How could they not see? How could they not believe?

When her mother had come to America in 1920, she had been only seventeen. A picture bride. Even then she had been a Christian, taught by the missionaries in Japan. But her father still practiced the Shinto religion. Keiko shook her head. Never would she ally herself with a non-Christian. Watching her mother's heart break little by little had hardened her own resolve. No, she would never marry a non-Christian.

She got to her feet, studying each doll as she did so. Most of the dolls were her mother's, but Keiko had added several of her own. As with her mother's dolls, each one held memories for Keiko.

She grinned at the little Kewpie doll that looked so out of place among the others with its bright red topknot. She had purchased it at the fair last year when she and her best friend, Sumiko, had gone. It had been so much fun.

She sobered, remembering how so many boys had followed Sumiko around. Even white boys were drawn to Sumiko's ethereal beauty.

The same could not be said of herself. She knew she wasn't ugly, exactly, but neither was she pretty. If she had to describe herself in one word, that word would be "ordinary." Except for one thing: By some accident of genetics, she was taller than most Japanese women. Compared to Sumiko, she felt like an amazon. And her nose tilted up on the end ever so slightly. Pushing a finger against the offending appendage, Keiko shrugged her shoulders. Oh well, there was nothing she could do about her height or her nose.

She made her way to the kitchen, trying to decide what to make for their supper that night. Sudden inspiration brought a sparkle to her eyes. Since Kenji would not be home, she would prepare her father a traditional Japanese meal and serve it to him in her kimono.

She grinned slightly. The kimono was not meant for comfort, but one day would not hurt anything. Besides, it gave her father pleasure to be treated in the old ways. She knew he didn't expect it of her, but it pleased him when she did.

Keiko picked up a porcelain teapot and turned to fill it. The screen door stood somewhat ajar from its last encounter with Kenji. Shaking her head, she reached over to latch it as she passed to the sink. She jumped back when a face suddenly appeared in her line of vision. The teapot shattered into tiny porcelain pieces as it fell at her feet.

She stared down in dismay, her heart slowing to a more reasonable pace. Glancing angrily at the man standing at her back door, she forgot to be afraid.

"Haven't you ever heard of using the front door! Now look what you've made me do!"

Brown almond eyes crinkled back at her. Although the stranger's lips twitched, his face remained serious.

"I apologize," he told her in flawless Japanese. "I already tried the front door, but I think that the bell is not working."

Undaunted, she continued to glare at him. "You could have knocked." Her sudden switch from Japanese to English seemed to surprise him. He pulled himself to his full height, which was considerable for an Oriental, and his narrowed eyes surveyed her from head to foot. Unlike Kenji, the stranger seemed to approve of what he saw.

"I did," he told her, his English as perfect as his Japanese had been.

Since Keiko had been in the kitchen, in all probability he was telling the truth. She couldn't have heard him if he had knocked softly.

Embarrassed, Keiko continued to stare at the stranger. She had never seen an Oriental so tall. And his hair curled softly around his head instead of hanging straight. It occurred to her then that he must be of mixed parentage.

"I am looking for Tochigi-san. Is this his house?"

"Hai." Instead of the short, staccato syllable, the affirmation came out in a soft drawn-out sigh. Color flamed into her cheeks, and her eyes went to the floor.

"He is my father," she informed him. "But he will not be home until later."

"My name is Shoji Ibaragi. I think your father is expecting me. Will you tell him I have been here and that I will return at. . ." He glanced at his watch. "Tell him I will return at six."

Remembering her manners, Keiko suddenly blurted out, "Come for supper."

He hesitated. "Are you sure? I do not wish to be any trouble."

"Hai." This time her voice was firm.

Bowing from the waist, he turned to go. Suddenly he turned back. *"Onamae wa?"*

Keiko dropped her eyes, the color once again blooming in her cheeks. "Keiko."

She wondered at the light that suddenly entered his eyes and the intense scrutiny he subjected her to, but he turned away too quickly for her to be sure of what she had seen. Relief?

"Sayonara." His voice drifted back to her as he rounded the house.

The rest of the day Keiko wavered between having a traditional meal as she had planned or making something more appropriate for company. Like roast?

Did Mr. Ibaragi like traditional Japanese food? Picturing him in her mind was easy. She could remember every detail about him, from his purely western clothes to his flawless Japanese. She was dying to know more about him, but that would have to wait until Papa-san came home.

Finally, Keiko decided on *sukiyaki* for supper and she saw no reason to change her plans where her father's guest was concerned. Probably she would never see Mr. Ibaragi again after tonight, so she might as well continue with her plans to please her father. Perhaps, in the back of her mind, was the thought that by pleasing him, he would not be so hard on Kenji.

Keiko could feel herself tense when her father came through the front door. He dropped the basket he used to carry vegetables to the market on the table by the door. She watched patiently as he took off his shoes and placed them in their cubbyhole in the *getabako*.

When he raised up, he noticed Keiko standing in the living room. His eyes gleamed when he saw her bright pink kimono. A small smile tilted his lips at the corner.

"Keiko-chan," he told her softly. "You are as lovely as your mother."

She knew that was not true. Her mother had been a beautiful woman, but she understood what he meant, and she was glad she had made the attempt to please him.

"Come, Papa-san," she told him, taking his arm and urging him to his favorite chair. "I have fixed some hot *ocha* for you."

She quickly retrieved the tea she had left in the kitchen on a tray. The old teapot reminded her of Mr. Ibaragi's visit.

"Papa-san, there was a man who called to see you. His name was Ibaragi. Shoji Ibaragi."

Her head was bent over the teapot, so she missed seeing her father's head shoot up and the color drain from his face.

"He was here?"

"Hai."

Keiko was alarmed at her father's sudden pallor.

"Did he say he would return?"

"Hai." Again her agreement was slow and drawn out. "I. . .I invited him for supper."

Her father's eyes grew wider. "Did he accept?"

"Hai. He said you were expecting him." It sounded more like a question.

Her father rubbed his face with his hands, his shoulders slumping. "Hai," he told her. "But I did not expect him so soon."

"Is there something wrong, Papa-san? Should I not have invited him?"

Slowly he shook his head. "No, nothing." Apparently forcing a smile, he studied her with loving eyes. "Sometimes I forget that you are growing up."

Frowning, Keiko wondered what that had to do with anything. She noticed how tired her father looked. How frail. Sometimes she forgot that he was getting older, too.

"Drink your tea, Papa-san. Mr. Ibaragi will be here at six."

Although Keiko had prepared a traditional Japanese meal, she set out the porcelain dishes on the dining table. She lay the chopsticks next to each place, wondering as she did so if Mr. Ibaragi would object to using them as Kenji would.

Her father had been so upset over the news of his arrival, Keiko had forgotten in her concern for her father to question him about the man. She remembered how his shirt and tie had accentuated his strong physique. Again she wondered about the size of him. He had towered over her.

When a knock sounded on the front door at precisely six o'clock, Keiko felt her heart lurch and her pulse begin to race. Her eyes went to her father, who was calmly walking toward the door. Nothing about him suggested anything other than casual interest.

Keiko waited in the entryway behind her father, but she couldn't see around the door her father held open. Her father was bowing low in the way only a true Japanese could do. His murmured greeting was too low for her ears.

Mr. Ibaragi stepped through the door and bowed as low as her father had. "Tochigi-san, *konban wa*."

His good evening held a wealth of respect, as had his bow. Keiko's eyes widened at the sight of him in his jeans mixed with the happi coat of the working man. On him the garment looked wonderful and not the least out of place. His tunic was tucked neatly in at the waist with a tie belt, the black silk highlighting the darkness of his skin.

Without being told to, Shoji leaned down and removed the shoes from his feet. When Keiko reached for them, his eyes met hers. Again there was something in their depths she didn't understand.

She followed them into the living room, watching as her father offered his guest the best seat in the house.

"Ibaragi-san, I had not expected you so soon," her father told him.

The young man bent forward, wrapping one hand around the other, draping them casually between his legs. His eyes were focused on the floor. When he finally looked up, there was such pain in his eyes that Keiko almost cried out to him.

"Tochigi-san, my father recently passed from this life. His final wish was that I come to you."

Keiko saw understanding in her father's eyes and sympathy as well. "I did not know. I am sorry to hear of this." He sighed gently. "We have much to discuss, Ibaragi-san, but for now let us share a meal. Come, Keiko is a fine cook."

Keiko looked at her father in surprise. It wasn't polite to brag on one's children, and her father rarely broke with decorum.

"Please, call me Shoji." His smile reached out from one to the other, and Keiko felt her heart give a thump so loud she was sure he must have heard it. Her face colored with confusion. Lifting her eyes to Shoji's, she found amusement lurking in their depths.

What was it about this man that could have such an impact both on her and her father? Her brow drew down in a frown. The man was a definite enigma.

She watched discretely as Shoji used his chopsticks proficiently. Her father gave her a broad smile and his eyes gleamed when she placed the dessert of hot apple cobbler in front of him. They exchanged smiles before Keiko handed Shoji his own serving.

"I hope you like apple cobbler, Shoji-san."

He smiled, his eyes warm. "It is one of my favorites, Tochigi-san."

Before she had time to answer, they could hear the back

door slam open. Kenji entered the room, his nose sniffing.

"Is that apple cobbler I smell?"

Keiko felt her father's frown before she saw it.

Rising quickly from her seat, she pushed her brother into his. "It is. Sit down and I'll get you some."

When she returned to the table, the tension in the room was thick enough to cut with a knife. Glancing at Shoji, Keiko found him watching father and son, a slight frown marring his features.

They finished dessert in silence. Keiko almost choked on her own. Why, oh why, couldn't Kenji and her father get along? Why couldn't her father see that he was driving Kenji away with his constant demands? And why couldn't Kenji see that her father only wanted his son's respect?

Kenji rose from the table, throwing his napkin on his plate. "I got homework to do."

Her father's frown increased. "Kenji-san, we have things to discuss."

"Look, Pop, I don't have time. I have an English lit test tomorrow."

"What I have to say will not take long. I need to speak with you both."

Kenji started to protest, but Shoji rose gracefully to his feet. "Perhaps I should leave."

Her father shook his head. "No, Shoji-san, this includes you, also."

Both Keiko and Kenji looked at the young man in surprise.

"Who is this guy?" Kenji demanded. "Whatta ya mean it involves him, too? What's he got to do with me?"

Instead of answering, her father turned and went into the living room, a clear indication that he didn't wish to discuss whatever it was in the kitchen.

Keiko followed her father with Kenji close behind. Shoji brought up the rear.

She sat down next to her father, her worried eyes begging her brother for tolerance. If there was one thing Keiko hated, it was conflict.

Shoji remained standing, arms folded across his chest, his face an inscrutable mask. Keiko finally understood what the term "inscrutable" really meant. There was no indication of embarrassment or anger or any emotion on his face. She had to admire his stoic countenance as she sat trembling from head to foot.

Keiko's eyes came back to her father when he cleared his throat. "Many years ago," he started, "I made a contract with a man I knew from Japan."

He stopped, unable to go on for a moment.

"What kind of contract?" Kenji demanded, glaring at Shoji. The inscrutable look never wavered.

Her father cleared his throat again. "Ibaragi-san was a good friend. We knew each other in Japan. We went to school together, until. . .until he went to the mission school. He later came to America and. . ."

Kenji began to fidget. "What kind of contract?" he asked again.

"A marriage contract between his first son and my first daughter, or my first son and his first daughter, whichever came first."

Kenji was on his feet in an instant. "Are you outta your mind? You must be if you think I'm marrying a girl I've never even met!" He shoved his hand through his slicked-back hair. "I can't believe even you would do such a thing!"

Keiko's eyes were on Shoji. He looked her way and for an instant his poise melted. His eyes were almost pleading. Only a moment, then the closed look returned to his face.

"He doesn't mean you, Kenji, do you?" she asked her father quietly, her eyes fixed on Shoji's. "Mr. Ibaragi has come for me, hasn't he?"

Kenji's eyes flew to Shoji's face. The truth was there for all to see.

"Get out!" Kenji hissed. "Get out before I throw you out!"

"Kenji!"

Never had Keiko heard her father's voice filled with such

authority. Kenji was silenced, but she knew it wouldn't be for long.

"You will not disgrace me before a guest in my home."

Keiko watched her brother's face contort with rage. "Me disgrace you! That's a laugh! You brought this disgrace on yourself!" Jerking his jacket from the coat rack in the hall, he headed for the door. "I'm outta here."

"Kenji!"

Ignoring his father's outraged voice, Kenji slammed the door behind him.

Still shaking, Keiko rose from her seat. "Father," she told him, using the title she so rarely used, "this is impossible, and you know it."

"Keiko," he pleaded. "I have given my word."

Turning to Shoji, she asked, "And what of you? Do you accept this arrangement?"

He hesitated only a moment. "I am willing to consider it. For my father's sake."

Keiko's eyes grew dark with suppressed fury. He may be an American, but obviously he had been raised in the old ways in Japan. It was bad enough to be considered as a wife for his father's sake, but to be told in so many words that she was being a disobedient daughter was more than she was willing to take from this man. Drawing herself up to her full height, she pinned him with a glare.

"Go back to Japan, Mr. Ibaragi, where you belong. I'm sure you will find a woman to accommodate you there."

She would have fled the room, but her father grasped her arm. "Please, Keiko, can we not discuss this?"

"No, Papa-san," she told him, hating the hurt look in his eye. "There is nothing more to discuss."

His shoulders slumped in defeat. Letting go of her arm, he took two steps before clutching his chest and suddenly pitching forward.

two

Shoji handed a cup of hot coffee to Keiko, who lifted tear-filled eyes to his face. She curled her fingers around the warm mug. She felt cold all over. Shoji stared back at her, wordlessly offering her sympathy and comfort. Between the two of them, they had managed to get her father into the farm truck and to the hospital.

Even if they had a telephone, it was unlikely an ambulance would have come that far, especially for a Japanese. Keiko was grateful that she had not been alone with her father since she did not know how to drive. If not for Shoji, Keiko wasn't sure what she would have done. But this would not have happened if he hadn't come.

Rage filled her like none she had ever known before. She turned away from his intense scrutiny, pretending to study the cold, stark hospital waiting room.

The hard-back chairs with their orange vinyl covers were something less than restful. The cold white walls made her shiver.

"Did you find Kenji?"

She jerked around, facing Shoji again. The anger bubbled just below the surface, waiting for an opening to allow an explosion. The only thing that kept her from lashing out at him was the remembrance of how gentle he had been with her father.

"No," she told him, looking away. "I left messages with all of his friends. That's all I can do for right now."

Nodding, Shoji sat down beside her. She pulled herself away as much as the seat would allow.

"Keiko, we have to talk."

17

She jumped to her feet, going to the room's only window.

"Can you not see that now is not the time?" In her agitation, she lapsed into Japanese.

Getting up, he crossed the room to her side. "I only wish to help," he returned, also in Japanese.

She rounded on him furiously. "Help! If not for you, none of this would have happened."

"I think you know that is not true."

At his soft-spoken words, she felt the air go out of her. It was true, what he said. She had noticed her father looking haggard over the last few months. She knew it had to do with the fact that the United States didn't allow issei to own property, since they were not American citizens.

Any property they "owned" had to be leased from nominees, and sometimes the nominees charged twice the going rate to rent the land. She knew that their landlord, Mr. Dalrimple, was not an honest man. But what could they do? Kenji wouldn't be twenty-one for another two years. When that happened, everything could be put in Kenji's name since he was a *nisei*, the American-born son of Japanese immigrants. But until that happened, they simply had to bide their time.

She knew the hard work and stress were taking a toll on her father, little by little. That and the fact that he and Kenji were constantly locked in conflict. Now. . .

A nurse walked into the room, breaking the silence that had lengthened to several minutes. Her eyes raked over Keiko's kimono, a curious glitter appearing in their frosty blue depths.

"The doctor will see you in a moment."

She left before Keiko could ask her any questions. Keiko and Shoji exchanged glances, returning to their silence.

Keiko moved away from the window and retreated to the safety of the only orange chair in the corner. The potted rubber tree somewhat obscured her from view. Being too close to Shoji made her very uncomfortable.

She watched him stare out the window, tall, strong, and

totally in charge of his emotions. She, on the other hand, was a bundle of nerves.

When the doctor entered the room, Keiko was the first at his side. Her worried brown eyes searched his face for some clue to her father's condition. Unlike the nurse, the doctor was gently sympathetic.

"I'm sorry," he told her softly, and Keiko felt her heart drop.

"Your father is in a coma."

Keiko's eyes went wide. "You mean, he's still. . .he's alive?"

When the doctor nodded, she took a deep breath. *Thank you, God! Oh, thank you!*

"He's had a heart attack, as I'm sure you've surmised." He hesitated. "His condition is not good. Physically we've done all we can for him, but. . ."

Shoji spoke for the first time. "But what, Doctor?"

"It's almost as though he has no will to live." He looked from one to the other, as if hoping they could enlighten him.

Keiko sucked in her bottom lip, as she eyed Shoji. Could her father not face his "shame"? To an issei, a debt of honor would be a matter of life or death—not something to be taken lightly by one's children. Keiko had never understood the issei rigidity when it came to matters of principle. Or was it even more than that?

"May I see him?"

The doctor hesitated. His look went from one to the other. Sighing, he crossed his arms. "Yes, but only for a minute."

Keiko looked down at her father lying so still and small against the starched white sheets. She flinched at the intravenous drip attached to his arm.

She stroked a hand gently across her father's forehead, bent, and kissed him gently. The tears began again.

"Can I stay with him tonight?"

The doctor shook his head. "I'm afraid not. It's against hospital policy. Besides, there's nothing more you can do for him tonight. I don't foresee him awakening from this coma for some time, if. . ."

He bit off the last word, but Keiko knew what he meant to say. If ever.

"You need to get some rest yourself," he told her gently.

Shoji took the coat from her arms and held it out for her. When she slipped her arms through the sleeves, he held onto her shoulders, squeezing gently.

Angrily she pulled herself away, hurrying across the room and down the hallway. She knew Shoji was right behind her, but she didn't really care. Suddenly she was weary beyond endurance. She wanted to crawl into her own bed and cry the tears that were threatening release.

She was waiting in the truck when Shoji slid into the driver's seat. He looked at her a long moment before starting the truck. The truck growled as he shifted the tired gears and pulled out of the hospital parking lot onto the desolate road out of town.

Over the rumble of the engine, Keiko sensed the waves of anger and frustration emanating from Shoji and she swallowed hard. It suddenly occurred to her that she was alone with a man who thought she was his future bride.

Glancing his way, she found his dark almond eyes glittering at her in the darkness. His jaws clenched tightly as he turned his gaze back to the road.

When they pulled up in front of her house, Keiko reached for the door, anxious to escape. Shoji's hand came down over hers.

"Wait."

He eased his tall frame from the truck, walked around the front, and opened her door. He reached a hand up to help her from the vehicle, but when she placed her hand into his, she was unprepared for the jolt of excitement that flashed through her.

Jerking her hand away, she quickly headed for the house. When she turned around, he was right behind her.

"Thank you for bringing me home and for helping with my father." His eyes never left her face as she stammered to a halt.

"Keiko," he admonished softly, "I told you we needed to talk."

"I'm too tired," she snapped. "And too upset."

He sighed. "You are not making this easy," he told her.

Shoving back the hair that had fallen from its bun, she continued to glare at him. "I have nothing to say to you. Any conversation you have will have to be with my father."

There was a strange gleam in his eyes that she didn't understand, but she took a quick step backward.

"Fine," he agreed. "Where do I sleep?"

"Excuse me?" Her eyes searched his features for some sign of understanding. "Gomen nasai?" she repeated in Japanese.

His lips twitched slightly. "Your father invited me to stay here."

Her eyes rounded in alarm. "You can't stay here! We're. . . we're. . ."

"Alone. I know," he finished for her. "But I can't walk back to town now. It's too late."

"Walk?" Her eyes searched the yard, but there was no sign of a vehicle anywhere.

"You walked?" she asked him incredulously.

"Hai."

"But. . .but. . .that's fifteen miles!"

"Hai."

She ground her teeth in frustration. "Is that all you can say?"

"Iie." His grin was infuriating. "No," he repeated as though she couldn't understand Japanese. "Keiko," he implored patiently. "May we go inside and talk about this?"

"Iie!" she snapped back at him. "You can't stay here. Neither my brother nor my father is here. We can't stay here alone."

"We are engaged," he told her softly. At the instant flash of fire in her eyes, he sighed again. "I didn't mean it like that."

"Well, however you meant it, you're not staying here."

Shoji rubbed his forehead with his hands, dropping them lamely to his sides. "May I sleep in the truck?"

Keiko stared at him in surprise. "What?"

His eyes held hers for a long time. "The truck. May I sleep in the truck? That way I will be here to drive you to town in the morning. You do wish to go to the hospital?"

Keiko would have denied him if she could have. Biting the corner of her lip, she wavered back and forth in her mind the advisability of doing as he asked. Surely Kenji would come home before morning. But what if he didn't? She simply had to get into town and see her father. *I have got to learn to drive.*

"Okay," she told him and saw his shoulders slump with relief. "Wait here and I will get you some bedding."

When she returned, she saw that he hadn't moved from the same spot she had left him in. He turned to her, taking the pillow and blankets from her hands. When he looked back at her face, his brown eyes were velvety soft in the moonlight.

"Oyasumi nasai," he told her softly.

"Good night," she repeated and watched him walk back to the truck and climb in the front. She shivered slightly, pulling her coat tightly around her. Maybe she should have let him stay in Papa-san's room. She knew without a doubt that he would be mortified if he knew how she had treated his honored guest.

Sighing, she went inside and shut the door. It was cold tonight. March in Southern California was still a little cool for camping out in trucks.

Gritting her teeth, she pushed such thoughts from her mind. He could very well look after himself. Anyone who would walk fifteen miles. . .no wait, forty-five miles. . .well, he could look after himself, that's all.

When she finally lay in her bed, she could no longer keep the thoughts at bay. *Lord, what do I do now?*

Was she the cause of her father's attack? She knew how traditional he was. Had her refusal to honor his contract made him lose face to such an extent that his heart couldn't take the strain? It was ridiculous, and yet. . .

God, help me. Tell me what to do. But the only words that kept coming to her mind were from the book of Ephesians. "Children obey your parents in the Lord, for this is right."

She pressed her palms tightly against her temples in an attempt to ward off any more thoughts. Groaning, she rolled to her side.

I don't even know if he's a Christian, Lord. He's kibei. Born in America, but raised in Japan.

Since she hadn't bothered to ask, she knew she was being unfair. He had tried to talk to her.

Finally, exhaustion took its toll and she fell into a deep, dreamless sleep.

❧

The sound of Otomodachi crowing brought Keiko back from the dreamless realms of sleepland. She smiled slightly, remembering her father bringing the red bantam home.

"If you do your duty and wake me in the morning, then you will be my friend," he told the cock. So his name had become Otomodachi, because he had done just what was expected of him and her father considered him a trustworthy friend.

But was she doing what was expected of her? All the events of the night before came rushing back at her.

Flinging her quilt aside, she hurriedly dressed. How had Shoji fared the night? Guilty pangs of conscience followed her everywhere.

When she opened the front screen door, she found him sitting on the porch.

"*Ohayo gozaimasu,*" he greeted her, his eyes wandering over her, taking in her changed appearance. There was nothing in their inscrutable brown depths to tell her whether he approved of the change or not.

Her dress was typically American. It flowed past her knees from a gathered waist cinched by a black patent leather belt. The apple-blossom-pink material accentuated her complexion and the white Peter Pan collar brought out the brightness in her dark amber eyes, which were highlighted by the dark bangs across her forehead. Her black hair hung straight and silky down her back.

Shoji had removed his happi coat, leaving only the black turtleneck beneath. The material hugged his body, allowing one to see the muscles that were so evident. Again Keiko marveled that an Oriental could be so large.

"Good morning," she returned his greeting. "Would you like some breakfast?"

"If it is no trouble."

"*Iie*, it is no trouble. Come inside."

Shoji followed Keiko into the kitchen wondering at the change in her. From traditional Japanese to typical American. Which was the real Keiko? It was important for him to find out.

"I like the dress," he told her and hid a smile at her evident embarrassment. "But I like the one you had on last night as well."

She glanced at him briefly as she filled their plates. "I only wear my kimono on special occasions. I much prefer the comfort of American clothes."

One eyebrow quirked upward, but he said nothing. He wondered if the inference meant that she would not live in Japan. Keiko laid a plate of eggs and toast in front of him.

"I'm sorry it's not more, but I'm rather anxious to get to the hospital."

"It is enough. *Arigato*."

"You're welcome."

Shoji bowed his head in thanks. *Father, bless this food and let it strengthen Keiko in this difficult time.* When he looked up, he saw Keiko's eyes wide in surprise.

"It is good," he told her, and her face flushed as she dropped her eyes to her own plate.

Shoji watched Keiko push her food around on her plate. He knew she must be desperate to know if her father was all right.

"You need to eat," Shoji admonished. "We have no idea what to expect, but you should do it on a full stomach."

Keiko choked down as much as she could, but in the end she left most of it on her plate.

୭

The hospital was more crowded than it had been the night before. People hurried to visit their family members, mindless of anything else.

Keiko was no different. She hurried to the nurse's desk to find out her father's condition and where they had bedded him. The nurse pointed them in the right direction, but asked them to wait until she could summon the doctor.

When the doctor arrived, Keiko was distressed to find it was not the same man as last night. His eyes were colder, and his attitude was one of impatience.

"Miss Tochigi?"

"Yes. My father. . ."

He stopped her with an impatient jerk of his head. Motioning to the waiting room, he frowned down at her. "Could we speak in here?"

Keiko was comforted by Shoji's presence standing so near. For some reason, this doctor frightened her. When Shoji put a large hand against her back, she made no objection.

"Your father is still in a coma," the doctor told her bluntly. "At this point we have no idea when he will come out of it, or even if he will."

The cold statement left her speechless.

"Where is he?"

Although Keiko could detect no change in Shoji's demeanor, she could hear the anger laced through his voice. Her eyes went to his, but they were as fathomless as ever.

Obviously the doctor sensed the same thing for his attitude altered slightly.

"I'll show you the way," he told them stiffly.

When Keiko entered the room, she saw her father as she had seen him the night before, only looking more frail than ever. The doctor last night said that they had done all they could medically, but that her father seemed to want to die. Could this be true?

He couldn't die! He just couldn't! He didn't know the Lord. He wasn't ready.

She knelt by the edge of the bed, taking his small hand into her own. Bowing her head, she began to frantically petition the Lord on his behalf. A hand on her shoulder brought her eyes around.

"I will leave you alone with him. If you need me, I will be in the waiting room."

She should be grateful for his support, but instead she was aggravated by it. He had no right to be here. This had nothing to do with him. But wait. Didn't it? Maybe she didn't think so, but she knew that being raised in Japan, he would have a whole different concept of honor. He would abide by his father's wishes no matter what his feelings in the matter.

A kibei! *Oh, Lord, I can't marry a kibei. I would be nothing but a slave.*

She could feel her father's weak heartbeat through her fingers. She didn't know how long she knelt there praying and petitioning, but she finally came to terms with herself. She knew what she had to do. She couldn't let her father die.

"Papa-san," she whispered softly. "Papa-san, can you hear me? Please Papa-san, come back to me. I need you." His breathing remained shallow, but she thought she detected a slight movement of his eyelashes.

"Papa-san, if you come back to me, I will honor your contract and marry Shoji."

Was she daring to tell a lie? No! She would marry Shoji. She just hadn't mentioned when. Maybe in fifteen years or so.

Guilt washed through her. No matter how hard she tried to justify it, she knew she was trying to be deceitful. Groaning, she dropped her head to the sheets beside her father's hand.

"I will marry him, Papa-san. I will," she whispered softly.

She jerked in surprise when she felt a hand on her shoulder. Shoji. It unnerved her the way he moved around so silently. She never heard him approaching, he just appeared. Had he heard her declaration? She looked into his eyes and realized that he had. For the first time, their fathomless depths were alive with his feelings, but she could not interpret them.

He lifted her from the floor. She wanted to protest, but she was just too tired.

"Kenji-san is in the waiting room," he told her softly. Her heart dropped at the announcement. She didn't think she was up to handling a confrontation now.

"How long has he been here?"

"About an hour." Her eyes widened in surprise.

"Why didn't you tell me sooner?"

He shrugged his broad shoulders. "We had a long talk."

"About what?"

"Things," he told her, making her grit her teeth in frustration. "He wants to see his father."

Keiko glared back at him in response. "No! I won't allow him to upset Papa-san."

"Keiko-san, he has as much right as you to see his father."

"I didn't run out on him!"

"Keiko-chan."

The soft croak from the bed brought her whirling to encounter the tired, pale face of her father. Although he was pale and drawn, there was a sparkle in his eyes. Tears filled her eyes.

"Papa-san, oh, Papa-san!" She flung herself to her knees, cradling his hand against her cheek. "You have come back. Thank God." The relief that washed through Keiko was palpable.

Her father's small brown eyes went from one face to the other. A slow smile spread across his features. Holding out his other hand, he took Shoji's hand and joined it with Keiko's, his own hands closing around their clasped ones. There was joy in the look he bestowed upon them.

Keiko felt her heart still, then thunder on. Had her father heard her declaration after all? Was it possible that that was what had rallied him? It couldn't be possible! Not so quickly.

"I wish to see Kenji-san," he told them weakly.

"Hai, Papa-san," she answered him softly.

Shoji again helped her to her feet, but her eyes refused to meet his.

"I think we should tell the doctor first," he told her, his voice little more than a whisper.

When Keiko agreed, Shoji went from the room to inform the doctor of her father's changed condition and to bring Kenji.

Kenji was the first to arrive, his face white and pinched. His eyes met Keiko's.

"I only found out this morning."

She bit back the comment she wanted to make. Now was not the time.

Kenji went to the bed, taking a closer look at his father. If anything, his face became paler.

"Papa-san, I am sorry," he told him in halting Japanese.

Their father's eyes twinkled back at him. "That is what I wished to tell you," he said. "I have been wrong Kenji-san."

He stopped, frowning back at his son. "I mean, Ken."

Keiko could tell how much it had cost him to call Kenji by the shortened American version of his name that he preferred. It had been a battle between them since Kenji had been about fifteen.

Kenji bit his lip, taking his father's hand into his own. "No, Papa-san. I am the one who is sorry. I have not been a very good son. If we had lost you now. . ."

Keiko felt her tears come again as she watched her brother struggle with his.

"For you, and only you, I will always be Kenji."

Their father's tired smile was reward enough. A minor battle won by compromise. Perhaps there was hope for their future after all.

A look passed between Kenji and Shoji, who had entered the room in time to hear this last bit of conversation. Keiko frowned. What had happened between the two that they seemed to suddenly be bosom buddies?

After the doctor examined their father, he looked from one to the other.

"I don't know how to explain it. I really hadn't expected him to recover."

Keiko was appalled at the doctor's insensitivity, and again she could sense Shoji's anger, though there was no visible sign.

"Perhaps we have more faith than you," Shoji told the doctor, and Keiko's eyes widened at the thread of steel in his normally soft voice.

The doctor looked uncomfortable. "Yes, well, I have other patients to see."

They waited until he exited the room and then they all began to talk at once. Mr. Tochigi lay weakly back against the pillow, smiling tiredly at his children. All three of them.

three

Keiko stared out over the garden, her thoughts were in turmoil in contrast to her peaceful surroundings. Basically, she had agreed to marry Shoji Ibaragi. She closed her eyes tightly, feeling helpless.

Although her father was doing better, he was still not out of danger. He had suffered some minor spells of irregular heartbeat and the doctors were keeping him under close watch.

He had insisted that Shoji have his room until his return, hopefully in a few days. In return, Shoji agreed to help Kenji run the farm until their father came home from the hospital.

When Shoji appeared at her side, she was unsurprised. She had expected him.

"I always promised myself that I would marry a Christian," she told him quietly.

She chanced a glance at him and found his inscrutable almond eyes staring solemnly back at her.

"What makes you believe that I am not a Christian?"

She stared at him in surprise. "Are you?"

He leaned on the porch rail, his eyes focused on the pagoda-roofed *kasuga* lantern in the far corner of the garden.

"I am."

Keiko frowned. "That doesn't make sense. A Christian wouldn't force someone to marry them."

He snorted softly, turning to her. There was an angry sparkle in his normally mysterious brown eyes.

"No one is forcing you, Keiko. I came here willing to fulfill my father's contract to your father, but I had no intentions of forcing you to do the same. That choice is yours."

She wanted to think about what he said, but he continued.

"Frankly, I am pleased with what I have found. I was unsure what kind of girl I would find."

The trepidation in his voice brought a sudden grin to her face. "What did you expect?"

He shrugged, for the first time looking uncomfortable. Keiko thought that he wasn't going to answer, but his voice came back to her, even and low.

"I had this vision of a girl with bobbed hair, thick makeup, and a tight-fitting dress."

Keiko laughed out loud. "And instead you found a rather dull-looking girl in a bright pink kimono."

His look was curious. "There's nothing dull about you. Why do you belittle yourself?"

Keiko flushed. In fact, she had been picturing Sumiko, her best friend. She was everything Shoji had just described, and yet she had beauty that Keiko would die for.

"I have seen for myself that you would make a fine wife." Her face colored crimson at the compliment, but he ignored her embarrassment and continued. "I think we can learn to. . . to care for each other."

"Like my parents," she answered him softly, refusing to look him in the face.

"Hai," he agreed. "I am willing to give you time. . .to give us time to get to know each other. Is this agreeable to you?"

When she didn't answer him, he lifted one of her hands into his. "Look at me, Keiko."

Slowly, hesitantly, she turned to him.

"Is there someone else?" he wanted to know.

Keiko would have laughed, but it wasn't funny. The only time men wanted to get close to her was when they wanted to be introduced to Sumiko.

"No, there is no one."

"Then will you agree to be engaged to me?"

If he had said the word "wife" she would have turned him down flat, but somehow the thought of being a fiancée was not as disturbing. It seemed less final somehow. Besides, what choice did she have?

"Hai." Her throat was tight with tears. When she turned away, he pulled her gently back. His hands curled softly around her upper arms.

"Keiko."

The command in his voice brought her eyes swiftly to his.

"We can make this work," he told her, pulling her inexorably closer. She read the intent in his eyes and felt a little thrill of fear. She would have turned away, but it was already too late. His lips closed over hers, warm and purposeful.

Frozen in time, Keiko felt a small flicker of response that suddenly burst into flame. She returned his kiss with a passion that surprised her.

Shoji slowly released her lips, pulling back, from her slightly. Keiko saw the frown on his face and felt her own crimson with embarrassment and shame. She had been too forward. It was not like her. Sumiko might perhaps get away with acting that way, but it was not like Keiko. What had gotten into her anyway?

Turning, she fled. This time Shoji didn't try to stop her.

Shoji slid one hand behind his neck, leaned back, and exhaled slowly. That was certainly unexpected. Actually, he wasn't sure just what he had expected to happen, but it certainly wasn't Keiko warm and responsive in his arms. He had meant the kiss to comfort her, to help her see that they would be a good match.

Confused, he slowly dropped his hands to his side. Who was this girl anyway? She had so many faces to her, he couldn't begin to understand the real Keiko. If he wasn't careful, he could wind up doing something they both would regret.

He sauntered down the steps, taking the path to the corner of the garden where a small pond was fed by a little waterfall. He crossed the bridge that led across it and seated himself on the stone bench next to the Japanese lantern.

For a time he watched the koi fish darting to and fro, their orange and white bodies bright against their dark background. Trapped. The creatures didn't even know that they were. Like him.

He watched the fish longer and began to realize something. They were quite content with their little world. They were well fed, well tended, and had a place of their own.

Leaning his head back against the wooden fence, he closed his eyes. Shouldn't he be content, also? Didn't the apostle Paul say to be content in all circumstances?

Keiko was a wonderful girl, a Christian even. She would honor and respect him all the days of their married life. What more could he desire?

Love. No matter how much he tried to push it away, the thought kept returning to him. He had always dreamed of having a marriage like his parents had shared for over twenty-seven years. Loving and devoted, he yearned for such a relationship.

"Papa-san, how could you do this to me?" The whispered words drifted upward to where he knew his father resided.

It didn't make sense. His father had loved the Lord, loved his mother, loved his marriage. How then could he have arranged a loveless marriage for his only son and expected Shoji to abide by it?

No matter how he looked at it, it still didn't make sense. He didn't think it would be hard to love Keiko, but that was beside the point.

He went back into the house, passing Keiko doing the dishes in the kitchen.

"Do you need some help?"

Her eyes opened wide and Shoji smiled.

"I may be *kibei*, but I have a thoroughly American mother. I assure you, I do not think women are here merely to serve me. If I was taught that way, my mother would have disabused me of that notion very quickly."

At her curious look, he grinned. "Of course, it seems a perfectly good way to me if you should choose to believe in it."

She gave an unladylike snort. "Don't hold your breath."

Laughing, Shoji picked up a dish towel and started to dry the plates. "You are a very good cook," he told her. "Did your mother teach you?"

She shrugged. "Mostly, although I learned a lot in Home Ec in high school."

"Such as?"

"How to care for the home, mostly. Sew. Things like that."

"A most worthwhile occupation," he told her, testing the subject.

She ignored the bait. "What of you? What occupation do you hope to attain?"

"For right now, I am a farmer."

Before she could comment, he laid the towel aside. "I think I will go to bed now. Good night."

When he reached the doorway, she called his name. He turned back to her, one eyebrow raised in enquiry.

"Father's room is comfortable for you?"

He grinned. "Hai. I have slept on a futon for years."

She shook her head disparagingly. "The rest of the house has mainly American furniture, but Papa-san had to have his room like the old land. He feels more at home in that room than in any room in this house."

Shoji glanced around. "I am impressed with the way you manage to combine the two cultures in your decorating."

He smiled slightly and left.

Keiko finished the dishes and turned out the light. Climbing the stairs, she made her way to her room in the dark. She was reaching for the lamp beside her bed when she heard a car coming down the road to the farm. It seemed to be coming at a high speed, spitting up gravel as it came.

Her first thought was that something had happened to her father, but then she realized that that was foolish. No one from the hospital would come racing out here and especially not at this time of night—unless it was Kenji.

Racing down the stairs, she flung open the front door and hurried down the porch steps to stand in the yard. Her heart was pounding.

The car pulled to a stop almost twenty feet away, its headlights blazing into her eyes. Keiko cupped a hand across her eyes, peering into the darkness.

"Kenji?"

Ribald laughter met her call and Keiko realized that the people in the car were not friends. She thought she recognized the driver from her high school, but she couldn't be sure.

"Hey, *geisha* girl," one drunken voice shouted. "Why don't you go back to Japan where you belong?"

Hoots of laughter greeted this statement. The driver's door opened.

"Better yet," the boy stumbling from the vehicle called. "Whyn't ya show me what you *geisha* girls can do?"

Yells of encouragement followed him from the car. Keiko felt real fear as she watched the boy stumbling toward her. She should have run, but her feet were frozen to the spot.

When the boy was less than ten feet away, Keiko saw a form blocking her view.

"Go inside," Shoji commanded.

"But. . ."

"Now!"

Keiko fled to the porch, but stopped there. When she turned back, Shoji was face to face with the boy from the car. In the headlights of the car she could see the boy's stupefied expression.

He had to look a long way up to see Shoji's face. Obviously unprepared for such an encounter, he began to back away.

"Who're you? You're not Kenji."

"If you don't turn around and leave, I'm going to become

your worst nightmare."

Keiko realized it was no idle threat. It seemed the boy must have realized it, too, because he began to slowly back up, his eyes never leaving Shoji's face. The boy was probably seeing double and one angry Shoji was frightening enough.

The boy climbed back into the car, throwing it into gear. The tires spun, throwing more dirt and gravel as he backed up.

"Go home, Tojo."

With that parting shot, he sped back down the dirt road. Keiko came slowly down the steps, coming to stand at Shoji's side. He was still staring after the car, his face once again an inscrutable mask.

"Has this happened before?" he asked her.

She shook her head, wrapping her arms tightly around her waist. "No. Never."

His eyes came to rest on her frightened face. He watched her a moment before he pulled her into his arms, giving her some of his body heat. She stayed there a minute, letting her legs regain some of their stability. Realizing that Shoji was standing there with nothing but his jeans on, she pulled away.

"You will catch your death out here. Come back inside."

He followed her back into the house. They seemed to have one mind, realizing that there would be no sleep for either of them until Kenji returned.

"I'll make us some tea."

When she reached the kitchen, she collapsed against the counter. She knew there was a lot of dislike for the Japanese, especially since they had invaded China and were helping Hitler. But she had not experienced very much herself. At least only what she considered the normal. Usually they were excluded from school functions, or the ones they were allowed to attend were routinely divided.

She felt the stirrings of anger at the injustice of it all. I am an American citizen just like they are. She even had the best scores in her class. When it came to scholastics, no one was superior to her. Yet they were still treated like outcasts. No matter what they did, how they dressed, how they acted, they would never be accepted.

She was still burning with anger four days later when they brought her father home from the hospital. Although many of the nurses were kind, there was still that attitude of superiority.

Sumiko was waiting on the porch when they pulled Kenji's car into the drive. She grinned, waving excitedly.

"Welcome home, Papa-san."

Keiko smiled. Long ago Sumiko and her father had adopted each other. When she turned to introduce Shoji, she found him staring at her friend, his enigmatic eyes giving away nothing of his feelings.

"This is Sumiko Shimura. Sue, this is Shoji, my. . .a friend of the family."

Shoji's gaze came to bear on Keiko's flushed countenance, thereby missing Sumiko's look of awe. Kenji hadn't missed it, though, and his lips turned down in a frown.

Shoji's look seemed to say, "That's what I was expecting of an American girl."

Keiko hid a grin. Sumiko's hair was bobbed close to her scalp, little pieces curling becomingly on her cheeks. Eyeliner added to the slant of her eyes, a touch of blue shadow brightening her dark brown orbs. Full red lips stretched into a flirtatious smile as she held her hand out to Shoji.

"Nice to meet you."

Without accepting the hand, Shoji bowed low in front of her. *"Hajimemashite."*

A quick frown replaced her fulsome smile. She stared from one to the other, before giving him a slight bow. Her perplexed look rested on Keiko. Taking pity on her friend, Keiko turned to Shoji. "Sumiko speaks very little Japanese."

Shoji's eyebrows flew up in surprise, his eyes traveling once more over Sumiko's form.

"I'm sorry," he told her in perfect English. "I am pleased to meet you."

The smile returned to her face. "And I am pleased to meet you." Curling her arm around his, Sumiko tried to lead him inside. He gently disentangled himself and turned to help Keiko's father.

"Tochigi-san, allow me."

Her proud father waved him away. "Surely you would rather spend your time with a pretty girl."

Keiko should have been amused, but instead she was aggravated by Sumiko's questioning expression.

"Oh, Papa-san. I am so sorry. Here, let me help you inside."

Brushing away Kenji and Shoji's hands, Sumiko helped Mr. Tochigi into the house. She brought him tea from the kitchen, knowing that Keiko would have it ready.

Smiling, Sumiko made sure Mr. Tochigi was situated before she turned to Keiko. "May I speak with you a moment?"

Keiko hesitated, but her father waved her away. "Go on. I am fine. Kenji-san and Shoji-san will keep me company."

Following her friend up to her bedroom, Keiko shut the door behind her. For some reason, she was reluctant to hear what Sumiko had to say.

Sumiko threw herself down on Keiko's bed. "I need your help," she told her without preamble.

Keiko's sense of dread increased. "What do you need?"

"I need to ask you a favor, but first, who's that hunk of Japanese manhood?"

Biting her lip to keep from grinning, Keiko tried to sound nonchalant. "I told you. He's a friend of the family's."

"Girl, why didn't you tell me you had a friend like that? Ooh, won't the other girls be as jealous as sin!"

Keiko frowned. "What do you mean?"

"Sister, you have yourself one of the best-looking jocks I've ever seen."

"I didn't say he was mine!"

"Well, if he's not, you'd better do something about that."

Shaking her head, Keiko smiled wryly. "You're incorrigible. What was the favor you wanted?"

Sumiko threw herself to her knees, her hands folded together in front of her. She looked like a cherub kneeling there in the middle of Keiko's bed.

"I want you to ask Kenji to take me to the school prom."

"What?" Keiko stared at her friend as though she had grown two heads. "Kenji?"

"Please, please, please, please, please."

Keiko giggled, shaking her head. "You're nuts, do you know that? Why can't you ask him?"

She snorted softly. "Like I would."

"If he knew you wanted to go, I'm sure he'd take you. He loves you like a sister."

Sumiko's smile vanished. She turned her face away, picking at the chenille bedspread.

"What is it, Sue?" Keiko asked softly.

"I don't want Ken to love me like a sister."

Keiko sunk slowly to the bed. "Oh, Sue. I didn't know."

She laughed without mirth. "I've loved Ken since we were six years old, when he punched that bully in the face for calling me a name."

Twisting her hands together, Keiko studied her friend. "What can I do?"

Sumiko turned her look back to Keiko, a serious glitter in her dark brown eyes. "This prom is my last chance, Kay. If I can't get him to see me as a woman, I'll be gone and it will be too late."

"Gone?"

"My father is sending me to San Diego to go to the university there. I leave next fall."

Keiko stared at her friend in disbelief. She couldn't remember a time when Sumiko hadn't been a part of their lives. She couldn't imagine not having Sumiko as part of her life.

"It's murder growing up!" Sumiko declared vehemently.

Silently, Keiko agreed. Everyone was growing older, including her father. Keiko pressed a hand to her forehead and started gently kneading it.

"I'll try," she told Sumiko. "But I can't guarantee anything."

"If he knows you're coming, too, he'll come. If for no other reason than to protect you."

It was true, Keiko knew. But she was almost equally sure Kenji would go to protect Sumiko. But, since Sumiko was not about to ask him, or anyone else for that matter, Keiko felt pushed against a wall.

Sumiko leaned forward excitedly. "I know. Ask Shoji."

"What?"

"You said he was a friend of the family. Surely if you ask, he'll go." Sumiko saw the hesitation on Keiko's face. "Please! I'll be your friend for life!"

She threw herself from the bed, kneeling at Keiko's feet. "Please! I'm begging you!"

Keiko started laughing, pulling her hand from Sumiko's grasp. "Oh, get up, for heaven's sake."

Sumiko continued to stare at her with those pleading brown eyes. Heaven help her brother if he ever fell in love with this girl, Keiko decided. No one could resist those eyes. She would be spoiled rotten. No wonder her parents doted on her.

Keiko rolled her eyes to the ceiling, heaving a great sigh. "Oh, all right. I'll try."

Squealing, Sumiko threw her arms around Keiko's neck. "I love you, I really do!"

"Yeah, right." Still, it felt good to make her friend so happy.

She would have to set Shoji straight in case he thought she was asking him to the prom for herself.

four

The brightly spinning ball in the center of the room reflected the lights of a thousand tiny prisms. As usual, Japanese Americans were on one side of the room, white Americans on the other.

Keiko's eyes went to Shoji. She felt again the thrill she had first experienced when she had first seen him in the black tuxedo, white shirt, and black silk cummerbund. He was so compellingly handsome, yet it was not his looks so much as his air of aloofness that made him seem so alluring.

A dark curl from his hair dipped tantalizingly across his forehead. Keiko's hand ached to push it back for him, but she hadn't the courage. Frowning, she mentally chastised herself.

She had seen the same look of awe in Sumiko's face that had been there the first time they had met. The message in her eyes was clear. *You better nab this guy before someone else does.* If she only knew!

Kenji stood beside Sumiko, one hand possessively at the small of her back. Sumiko's triumphant look brought a small smile to Keiko's face. It seemed Sumiko had her wish. From the moment Kenji had laid eyes on Sumiko in her sleek, gold silk dress, something subtle had changed in their relationship.

Sumiko's dress hugged her curvaceous figure like a second skin. It made Keiko uncomfortable. As a Christian, she could never countenance such an unlikely outfit. It seemed to have one purpose, and that was to shout to the world "Here I am."

Her own chiffon dress flowed around her in soft, billowing folds. Its pale blue color added a soft radiance to her face that she was unaware of.

Keiko tried not to notice Shoji's eyes as they followed her

and the look of silent wonder in their dark brown depths.

"Sumiko."

The four of them turned at the sound of a slightly slurred voice behind them. Keiko almost dropped her glass of punch when she was confronted by the youth who had accosted her in their driveway just a few weeks before.

She glanced at her friend, wondering at their relationship. Sumiko's eyes had gone suddenly cold, her face becoming a haughty mask.

When Keiko turned to Shoji, she realized that he had recognized the boy, also. As he was the last time, so he was now—drunk, though not as far gone as that night.

Shoji's eyes darkened to obsidian as the boy's eyes roved boldly over Sumiko before turning to Keiko.

"Hey! It's the *geisha* girl!"

"Why you. . ."

Keiko grabbed her brother's arm. "Not here, Kenji."

The boy only grinned, his cold blue gaze going from the top of Kenji's head to the polished toes of his shoes.

"Any time, any place, Kenji boy."

Sumiko pushed herself between them, one hand on each of their chests. Keiko had never seen her friend's eyes so cold.

"Go back to your girlfriend, John Parker. She's waiting for you."

The girl in question hovered uncertainly on the edges of the crowd that was forming.

"Let her wait." Embarrassed, the girl turned and fled at his belligerent response. John Parker's eyes grew serious, though his voice was still slightly slurred. "I wanted to talk to you," he told Sumiko, his voice taking on an irritating whine. "Why haven't you returned my calls?"

Kenji's eyes flew to Sumiko's face. She stared helplessly back at him, shrugging her shoulders.

"It's not what you think."

Before Kenji could make any kind of response, John's

friends joined him, their cold glances surveying the small group.

"Come on, John. Come back to the party."

John looked at Sumiko. "I'm not going anywhere until I have my dance with Sue."

"Over my dead body," Kenji raged. "You're drunk as a skunk and you're not fit company for anyone, much less a lady."

John ignored him, his eyes still on Sumiko's face. It was obvious that he intended to have his way. As the only child of the town's banker, John was hopelessly spoiled, believing himself above even the law. That much was obvious by his intoxicated state.

"Stay here," Sumiko commanded John, pulling Kenji to the side. They were at once embroiled in a heated debate that left Kenji smoldering while Sumiko returned to John.

"One dance, John, and that's it."

Kenji stormed off and Keiko watched him go with worried eyes. She turned a pleading look on Shoji.

"Will you go with him?"

Shoji's eyes had already followed Kenji's progress across the room. He shook his head.

"No, I will not leave you alone."

Her brows drew down in irritation. "I'll be okay. It's Kenji I'm worried about."

Taking her by the arm, he headed in the direction they had seen Kenji disappear. "Fine, then you can come with me."

They found Kenji sulking in the corner of the hallway outside the gymnasium doors. Dropping her arm, Shoji strode over to him, glaring at the younger boy.

"You would just leave your date?"

Kenji glared back at him. "What would you have me do? She made her choice."

Snorting softly, Keiko pinned her brother with frosty brown eyes. "She was trying to stop trouble before it started. You know that. What's one dance?"

Surging off of the wall, he gave her glare for glare. "I could have taken care of John Parker."

"Right! And how would you have done that? Fight?" Her scathing look caused him to flinch. "And where would that have gotten us? Think! For once in your life let your brain rule over your emotions."

She turned to stalk away only to encounter Shoji's amused expression. Gritting her teeth, she pushed her way past him and back into the gym.

It was only moments later that they followed her back. Keiko didn't know what Shoji had said, but it obviously affected her brother. Although he was sullen, he seemed more amenable.

The soft sounds of the Glenn Miller orchestra filled the auditorium through the speaker system. Without realizing it, Keiko began to sway slightly to the music. She loved his songs.

"Dance?"

Surprised, Keiko turned to Shoji. "You know how?"

Smiling, he took her into his arms and began to drift around the gym. Keiko's expression amused him. Bending down, he began to hum the music into her ear. She pulled back, her look eloquent.

"I think there's a lot about you that I don't know."

His smile turned into a full grin. "That makes two of us. I didn't know you had claws."

She knew he was referring to her encounter with Kenji.

"Remind me never to make you mad at me," he told her softly, pulling her closer in his arms.

Keiko closed her eyes and gave herself up to the pleasures of the music, and admittedly, Shoji's company. Shoji was an excellent dancer. Where had he learned to dance? His mother? Keiko was becoming increasingly curious about the woman who had raised such a son.

When the music ended, Sumiko returned to Kenji. Keiko

could tell there had been no pleasure for Sumiko in dancing with her antagonist. John could tell that, too. His brooding eyes followed Sumiko as she took her place on the floor with Kenji.

At first they were stiff in each other's arms, Kenji holding Sumiko at arm's length, but before long the soothing music helped ease the tension between them. Keiko saw them relax. When Sumiko smiled up at Kenji with those soulful brown eyes of hers, Kenji hadn't a chance.

Shoji followed her look, a grin forming on his handsome face. "Kenji will have his hands full with that one."

Keiko arched an eyebrow at him. "Oh?"

He slanted her a sideways look, one eyebrow cocked. "You know it's true. Aren't women the same anywhere? They pretend to submit, when all the time they make a man dance to their tune."

She was flabbergasted at his totally un-Japanese assessment of women. "Is that what you really think?"

"Keiko-san," he answered her softly. "I have already said more than I should have. I think it is time to dance." He grinned at what he had just said. "No pun intended."

As he pulled her onto the floor with him, Keiko lifted exasperated eyes to his. She opened her mouth to continue the argument, but he smiled down at her, causing her stomach to do flip-flops.

"Shhh," he told her, effectively ending the conversation.

Keiko was confused. Shoji was unlike any *kibei* she had ever known. No *nisei* girl of her acquaintance would willingly align herself with one. They were too Japanese in their treatment of women. Everyone knew that Japanese boys raised in Japan soon forgot their American heritage. How had Shoji been immune? Was it his mother's influence again?

To her way of thinking, it was much better to be *nisei*, a second-generation Japanese born and raised in America.

The *kibei* were more Japanese than American, and when they returned to America they expected the Japanese here to be the same.

All of the *nisei* girls that Keiko knew would be horrified if they knew that Shoji was *kibei*, not to mention that she was engaged to him due to their fathers' contract. Even Sumiko didn't know. As a *nisei* herself, Sumiko had been raised totally American. Unlike most *issei*, Sumiko's father had left Japanese ways entirely behind.

It had been her experience that most of the *issei* clung tenaciously to a way of life they knew. That's what caused so much resentment among the Americans, even to the point of denying them citizenship.

Keiko's chest swelled. Well, she was as American as anyone else. She had been born here in California, and she had been raised here in California.

Through a gap in the crowd she spotted John Parker standing on the other side of the gym. He was deep in discussion with his two buddies, but his eyes followed Sumiko wherever she went.

John's father was part of the Oriental Exclusion League, which probably accounted for much of John's antipathy toward the Japanese. Keiko wondered what John's father would say if he knew that John was in love with one.

Keiko could tell by Sumiko's rapturous expression that she was totally unaware of anyone except Kenji. For tonight, Sumiko was living her dream.

"You're very quiet."

Startled, Keiko turned her face up to Shoji. She had to look such a long way up. How tall was he? Six-four? Six-five?

"I wanted to thank you for coming with me."

One dark brow winged upward. "You didn't think I would allow my fiancée to come alone, did you?"

There was an almost aggressive note in his voice that caused Keiko's friendliness to slowly evaporate. She hated being reminded of the situation between them. If not for that, maybe they could have become friends, but as it was, every move was suspect to her. It was always in her mind that he was doing it because it was his duty and he would fulfill that duty to the best of his abilities.

A scuffle at the other end of the room brought them to a standstill. Kenji and John were in a heated argument, Sumiko trying her best to intervene.

Keiko tried to pull away, but Shoji held her still. "No, you stay put."

She rounded on him. "I will not! There's three against one!"

His eyes were fierce when he looked at her and Keiko felt a tingle of alarm. It was at times like this that Shoji was all kibei, and Keiko was more than a little afraid of him.

"I said stay put." Although his voice was soft, there was that in it that had the effect of freezing Keiko to the spot.

She watched him cross the room to where Kenji was surrounded by John and his two friends. He moved with such grace and quiet that the group never heard him approach.

John was the first to spot him. Keiko could hear his angry voice even from her position halfway across the gym.

"Get outta here, Tojo. This is none of your business."

Keiko couldn't hear Shoji's quiet response, but it must have held the same quality he had used with her because the crowd around them began to pull back.

Though Shoji was slightly taller than John's friends, it wasn't his height that was so frightening. It was that air of leashed violence that surrounded him at times. Keiko shivered, but not from being cold. That the others were frightened was obvious, though they made a show of being brave.

John shoved Shoji, but his body never moved. His feet were firmly planted. Keiko would have given all she owned to see his face at that moment. Were his eyes as inscrutable as they usually were?

When John threw a punch, Shoji lifted a hand so quickly he

was able to catch John's fist with it. He continued to hold it as John struggled for release. The whole time Shoji continued to speak to them.

Keiko envied Sumiko her location next to the scene. Her eyes were wide with the awe she revealed every time she looked at Shoji.

Kenji continued to argue heatedly. One look from Shoji and he was silenced. It was clear that Shoji was trying to avoid a fight. Perhaps if John's bravery hadn't had a little boost from alcohol, he would have heeded the message. As it was, he continued with his hostile tirade.

When one of John's friends grabbed Shoji from behind, Keiko felt herself loosed from the power of his influence. She was across the floor in seconds, but before she reached their position, she saw Shoji flip the boy across his shoulders. John and the other boy jumped to help, but they found themselves flat on their backs.

Keiko reached Shoji's side, her eyes going from one boy to the other. They got slowly to their feet, definitely losing some of their belligerence.

The largest of the boys lunged at Shoji again, but he stepped aside. The momentum carried the boy forward, and he found himself once again on the floor.

"That's enough." Mr. Collins, the school principal, descended on the group, his angry gaze fixing on Shoji. "What's going on here?" he demanded.

John brushed off his tuxedo without looking at the principal. "This guy attacked me. Mark, Stan, and I weren't doing anything when Kenji started a fight."

"That's a lie!" Sumiko's angry form planted itself in front of Mr. Collins. "John started it. He wouldn't leave me alone."

Mr. Collins stared at them all with disgust. His eyes came back to Kenji.

"What are you doing here, Kenji? You graduated over a year ago."

Sumiko answered for him. "He's my date."

"And you?" He looked rather uncomfortable when faced with Shoji's mysterious dark stare.

"He's my date," Keiko told him.

"I see." He looked from one to the other before turning back to Sumiko. "I think you and your dates had better leave."

"That's not fair!" Sumiko fumed. "Why should we have to leave when we didn't do anything?"

Mr. Collins' eyes became black in their intensity. "Would you rather be expelled?"

Sumiko's face drained of color. She and Keiko were only two weeks away from graduation.

"We'll go," Keiko told him, taking Kenji and Shoji by the arms.

Sumiko struggled with the desire to say more. Prudence won out and she turned away, but not before fixing John with such a look of loathing his eyes went wide.

Shoji helped Keiko into the back seat of Kenji's roadster, climbing in beside her. His look was thoughtful as he continued to stare at her.

Keiko felt herself squirm under his perusal. What was he thinking? As for herself, she had a lot to think about. How could she possibly marry a man who could frighten her half to death?

Shoji could be so gentle and kind, but there was always this air of ferocity that surrounded him. What would it be like if he ever became really angry? Her toes curled into her shoes at the thought. Heaven forbid.

Shoji opened his mouth to say something, but Kenji interrupted, his voice full of enthusiasm.

"Man! That was great! Can you teach me to fight like that? Was that judo?"

Keiko saw the closed expression come to Shoji's face even in the dark. The moon highlighted his features, making them seem cast in bronze.

"Yes, it was judo, and no, I will not teach you."

Kenji took his eyes off the road, turning to Shoji in surprise. "Why not?"

"It would take too long to explain. I'd rather not go into it now."

"But. . ."

"I said, not now."

Silence filled the car. What had started out as such a promising evening had turned into a fiasco. Keiko looked at Sumiko and noticed the tears slowly coursing down her cheeks.

When they reached the house, Keiko and Shoji got out of the car. Keiko squeezed her friend's shoulder before Kenji roared away. She was watching the car disappear down the road when she felt Shoji take her arm. Flinching, she pulled herself away.

His look was as inscrutable as ever. He followed Keiko into the house, but she went immediately to her room, closing the door firmly behind her.

Shoji sighed heavily as he heard Keiko's door close. When would he ever learn? Fighting was not an answer to anything. True he hadn't provoked the fight, but it had given him great pleasure to end it. It would have given him even more pleasure to have beaten those three thugs to a pulp.

Shoving the anger down inside, Shoji went to the kitchen and poured himself a glass of milk. He closed his eyes as he thought of that day so long ago.

A schoolmate had called him a name, and though they were all taught judo, Shoji's size gave him the extra edge he needed to conquer even the hardiest of school chums. That and his constant anger.

When Kenzo had attacked him verbally, Shoji had attacked him physically. Groaning, Shoji placed the glass back on the counter. He had wound up putting Kenzo in the hospital. A fourteen-year-old boy, and he had almost lost his life.

That's when it had been decided that Shoji needed extra guidance and he had been placed under the tutelage of a Chinese monk. Boy, how his mother had reacted to that one.

Still, Master Wong had taught him the art of self-control. At least to an extent. Never again did Shoji wish to do what he had done to Kenzo. Until tonight.

Shoji's father had told him that he was much like Jesus. Power under control. That's what his father had said was the true definition of meekness. It didn't mean being a doormat. It meant you knew you had the power to destroy and yet you controlled it.

Jesus' destruction of the temple and driving out the money-changers was nothing compared to what He could have done. Isn't that what He tried to show His disciples when He had cursed the fig tree? Only a word from His mouth and it was forever destroyed.

Jesus witnessed many injustices, but He held His wrath. That was for His Father to handle; that was not His purpose.

Just as it was not Shoji's purpose to punish those who hurt the people close to him. Judo was meant for defense and defense alone. Even the word itself meant "the way of gentleness."

Shoji rubbed his face with his hands. He had to get a handle on his temper. Even twelve years in Japan had not been much help.

Throwing back his head, he closed his eyes. The look on Keiko's face. He would never forget it. Such fear. How could he possibly undo the damage he had inflicted tonight? And what was worse, he was pretty sure there would be retribution from John Parker and his friends.

❧

Two months after the prom, it took all of Shoji's willpower to keep from throttling Keiko Tochigi. He gritted his teeth now thinking about it.

She was avoiding him as much as possible. When he entered a room, if she was alone, she quickly left. He tried to get her by herself several times, but she was adept at outmaneuvering him.

So far, he had been unable to apologize for that night. He sighed, slamming the shovel into the ground in his aggravation. This was definitely not what he had meant when he said they needed to get to know each other.

When he looked up, Keiko was coming across the field with a glass of lemonade. It was obvious from her face that it was not her own idea. She pulled up next to him and held out the glass.

Taking off his gloves, he reached for the drink, his eyes never leaving her face. She looked everywhere but at him. When he took the glass, she turned to leave, but he reached out a hand and took her by the arm.

She didn't flinch away from him like he expected. She merely stood with her head bent down.

"Arigato."

"You're welcome."

He continued to hold her arm, watching her face for some sign of the friendliness they had shared before. He knew she didn't hide her feelings well.

"Keiko, I want to apologize for the night of your prom."

Her head remained bent, her eyes focused on the ground. "You have nothing to apologize for. You only did what I wanted to."

When her eyes looked into his he saw a contriteness he hadn't expected. "I'm sorry for the way I have been acting." She turned her face away again. "It's not easy for me to apologize. I have a rather stubborn nature."

Surprised, he set the glass on the ground. Taking her by the arms, he turned her to face him.

"You want to apologize to me?"

She nodded. "I have been very inhospitable. Even my

father has noticed it."

He leaned back, still not releasing her. "Ah. So this was your father's doing."

"I. . .I wanted to apologize. I mean I. . ." She stopped, biting her lip. Her eyes clashed with his. "You frighten me, Shoji. There's something so. . .so. . .intense about you. You're so. . .unreadable."

He released her, but she didn't move away. "That comes from years of practice. If you want to know what I'm thinking, ask me."

She ducked her head again. "Maybe if I knew you better."

Shoji was careful to keep accusation out of his voice. "It has not been my fault that we still know so little about each other."

"I know." She smiled timidly up at him. "May we try again?"

He lifted the empty glass from the ground and handed it to her. He returned her smile. "I would like that."

Nodding, Keiko turned and left him standing there remembering how she looked the night of the prom. He watched her cross the yard before turning back to his work.

❧

August turned into September. October saw the end of the summer harvest. When November rolled through with its chill winds, Keiko planned a special Thanksgiving.

There was much to be thankful for, though anti-Japanese sentiment was growing progressively. Since her graduation, she had spent very little time in town.

When Sumiko went off to college, she was wearing Kenji's ring. This was one of Keiko's major reasons for thanks. Her father's health was improved, and the crops had been good. There was quite a bit of money in the bank.

Shoji was planning on taking Keiko to see his mother before Christmas. Just the thought of it sent fear spiraling through Keiko's midsection.

Although Keiko and Shoji had resumed their friendship, there had been very little time to get to know each other until now. She was unsure if she wanted their relationship to change. There was still that little niggle of fear that surfaced from time to time when she saw Shoji in one of his rare moods—usually when he returned from town with Kenji, whose face would be as black as a thundercloud.

Sundays were special days for Keiko, when she and Shoji would go together to church. Even Kenji had been cajoled into going a time or two.

On this particular Sunday morning, Shoji had borrowed Kenji's roadster, and Keiko was feeling euphoric after listening to a wonderful sermon by Mr. Kosugi. She tied a red silk scarf to her head, trying her best to keep the cold wind from whipping her hair into a frenzied mess.

Smiling, Keiko reached to turn on the radio. The strains of a Glenn Miller song drifted out to them, reminding Keiko of that night so long ago. She was about to turn it off, when an announcer broke into the music with a special message.

"The Japanese have attacked Pearl Harbor. I repeat, the Japanese have attacked Pearl Harbor."

Keiko froze with her hand outstretched. "It can't be," she whispered.

Shoji pulled to the side of the road and together they listened to the message. Death and destruction and untold damage to the U.S. fleet.

Shoji looked at her, his eyes unreadable. What must he be feeling? She didn't think now would be the time to ask.

"Let's go home." His voice was deathly quiet.

She nodded to let him know she agreed.

Surely this meant that now the United States would declare war on Japan.

Dear God! Dear God!

five

For the rest of the day, Keiko, Shoji, Kenji, and Mr. Tochigi huddled around the radio. The radio's continuation of its regular programming seemed oddly out of place against its periodic messages of devastation.

"I still can't believe it," Kenji declared in a tight voice.

"What will it mean for us?" Keiko wanted to know.

Her father shrugged. "We will have to wait and see."

Keiko wasn't worried for herself and Kenji. They were American citizens. It was her father that concerned her. She glanced over at Shoji. His eyes were focused on the radio, but she could tell he wasn't listening. He got up from his seat.

"I have some things to do."

Keiko watched him leave, realizing that he was in one of his dark moods. Swallowing hard, she followed him from the room. She found him in the garden pulling dead weeds from the flower beds. Kneeling down beside him, she began to methodically help.

"You're. . .you seem. . ." She didn't know how to continue and was a little afraid to do so.

Heaving a deep sigh, he turned to look at her. His eyes moved over her face, coming to rest on her lips, then back to her eyes. His were so fathomless she had no hope of reading into them.

"I told you all you had to do was ask."

She studied him intently. "I'm asking."

He sat down on the ground, wrapping his arms around his legs. Resting his chin on his knees, he seemed to be trying to get his thoughts in order.

"I have no idea of who I am! Never have, and I'm not sure

I ever will." His gaze focused on a bird in the pine tree in the center of the garden. "In Japan, I was an American. In America, I'm Japanese. But not really."

Keiko nodded understanding. As a *nisei*, she understood all too clearly the implications of dual nationality. His look returned to her.

"It's not the same with you and Kenji. You have been raised as an American, so at least you understand Americans. I, on the other hand, have been raised for the last twelve years in Japan. I understand their ways more than the American way, yet not fully."

Keiko remained silent, knowing that he hadn't finished. She could tell he was trying to find the right words to say.

"At least you and Kenji are full-blooded Japanese. I am mixed Japanese and white. I love my parents, but at times I have been so angry with them, I wanted nothing more than to never have anything to do with them. In Japan I was treated as less than nothing. In America I am treated much the same. I know what the *nisei* think of the *kibei*.

Eyes turned away, Keiko knew she couldn't deny it. Hadn't she thought much the same herself? For some reason, it hurt her to hear the pain in his voice.

"So you carry your anger around with you like a shield."

He pursed his lips, not looking at her. "I suppose."

Deciding to risk his wrath, she sat down close to him. "And what has Jesus done for you, Shoji?"

He smiled wryly at her. "I know what you are trying to say. It's something I have grappled with for many years. I love the Lord. I try to serve Him. But I can't seem to let go of the anger. I feel like a nobody."

Keiko's lips tilted at the corners. "Perhaps I should introduce you to my friend Anna."

"Anna?"

Keiko looked into his eyes, willing him to understand her. "Anna is a Christian, too."

His eyes narrowed, not following her.

"Her parents are Jews."

He leaned back, understanding written across his features. "And how does Anna deal with this?" he wanted to know.

Keiko smiled, throwing a weed on the pile that had been growing as they spoke.

"Anna says it doesn't matter to her. She is an alien no matter where she goes. Her citizenship is in heaven. So, she tries to help as many people as possible attain that citizenship, too."

"She sounds like a nice girl," Shoji commented softly.

"She is. But her parents have disowned her."

He frowned. "What does she do then? Who takes care of her?"

"She lives with a Christian family and works at their store. She keeps hoping and praying that someday she can win her parents to the Lord."

"Like you."

Keiko looked at him. Shrugging, she got up from the ground. "I have to fix supper."

"Thanks for taking the time to ask."

"Thanks for talking to me."

Keiko fixed supper, but no one was interested in eating. They had heard on the radio that towns along the western seaboard were preparing for an invasion. There was a blackout restriction as of seven o'clock.

With each broadcast, Keiko felt her heart grow heavier. It was evident that war was imminent. She watched her father, afraid the stress would cause another attack. Instead, he calmly rocked in his favorite chair, seemingly oblivious to the raging tide around them.

"Keiko-chan," he addressed her. "I would like to hear you read from your mother's Bible."

She jerked her head up in surprise, studying his face. Her brows creased with concern. Her father had never shown any interest in the Bible before. What was running through his mind? And why her mother's Bible?

She found out a few minutes later. Lifting her mother's Bible from the chest where it was kept for safekeeping, Keiko carried it carefully back to where her father sat. Although her father understood a lot of English, he had never learned to read it.

"Read any notes from your mother that you see."

The Book flipped open to Ephesians, seemingly of its own accord. Her father nodded solemnly as she read about unity in the body of Christ and living as children of light.

She had never read her mother's Bible before and hadn't realized how many notes she had written. The familiar handwriting brought tears to her throat.

When she read the part about wives submitting to their husbands, her voice faltered and then stopped.

"What is wrong, Keiko-chan?"

"Nothing, Papa-san. There is a note in the margin from Mother."

She hadn't realized that Kenji had been drawn into the reading until his husky voice penetrated her own musings.

"Read it," he commanded quietly.

Keiko hesitated. "It says. . .it says that a Japanese wife is taught this from birth."

Her father's eyes took on a decided twinkle. "There has to be more."

Keiko smiled wryly. "Yes. It also says that if Japanese men were taught the rest of those verses, marriage would be a heavenly thing."

Mr. Tochigi laughed aloud. "I knew she would have something to say on the matter."

He got up from his seat. "It is time for me to go to bed. It has been a long day. *Oyasumi nasai*."

Keiko smiled softly at him, her heart overflowing with love. "Good night, Papa-san."

Kenji rose to follow his father. "I think I will turn in, also. Good night."

Keiko and Shoji each added their good nights and watched her brother walk from the room.

"Keiko." Shoji's voice was soft, but compelling.

"Hai?"

"I do not wish for you to go into town for awhile. At least not until this blows over."

The seriousness of his expression warned her that he was in earnest. She was about to argue with him, then thought better of it. The only reason she wanted to argue was that she hated being told what to do. This was no time to be stubborn.

"Hai," she answered him softly.

He got up from the sofa, stopping when he reached her side. His hand extended, he stroked a finger across her cheek. Bending, he touched his lips lightly against her cheek.

"*Oyasumi nasai*, Keiko-chan."

Her eyes flew to his at the unexpected title of endearment. Keiko-san was a title of respect. Keiko-chan was used for someone dear. Her heart fluttered at the brooding intensity of his look.

"Good night." She didn't recognize the croak as her own voice.

That night when Keiko said her prayers, she included her country. What a mess men made of this planet. Why couldn't people learn to get along, especially the different races?

She knew the answer to that one. Sin. If not for that first sin, they would even now be living in a perfect world.

Angrily she thumped her pillow into a ball, burying her head into its soft down. "Thanks a lot, Eve," she mumbled into the darkness.

❧

The doorbell rang early the next morning, and Keiko hurried to answer it. She opened the door to a woman, not young but neither was she old. She had what Keiko had always called "class," her auburn hair beautifully coiffed and curled.

She smiled at Keiko. "Is this the Tochigi residence?"

"Yes." Surprised, Keiko temporarily forgot her manners.

"May I come in?"

Flustered, Keiko opened the screen door. "Of course. I'm sorry, please come in."

The woman moved inside, her glance carefully surveying the room. When she turned to Keiko, her beautiful blue eyes smiled warmly, though there was a hint of reserve behind their obvious friendliness. There was something vaguely familiar about the woman.

"What a lovely home."

"Thank you." More confused than ever, Keiko asked the woman to be seated.

She continued to look around with interest before her eyes returned to Keiko's face. Her smile was genuine, and Keiko felt herself relax slightly. There was something about this woman she liked.

"I suppose you're wondering who I am."

Before Keiko could reply, the door opened and Shoji and Kenji came in. They were brushing hay from their pants, laughing at some joke they had shared.

Shoji looked up and the smile froze on his face.

"Mother!"

The woman rose gracefully to her feet. "David, how are you?"

"David?" Kenji and Keiko questioned at the same time.

Shoji frowned. "Mother, what are you doing here?"

"David, where are your manners? I haven't been introduced."

Sighing heavily, Shoji turned to Keiko. "Keiko Tochigi, Kenji Tochigi. My mother, Mrs. Ibaragi."

"How do you do?" The woman's gracious smile was lost on Kenji.

"David?"

His mother looked perplexed. Shoji motioned for her to be seated.

"I haven't gone by David in years, Mother, and you know it."

"I don't understand." Keiko's puzzled glance went from one to the other.

"David Shoji Ibaragi," his mother intoned, her sweet smile resting on her son. "After King David, don't you know."

Shoji must have decided to use his middle name when he lived in Japan, Keiko decided. It made sense. He would be less likely to stand out as an American.

"You haven't been in touch with me since you arrived back in the states," Mrs. Ibaragi told her son, a decided edge to her voice.

He looked away. "I know. I would have called you soon."

"Be that as it may, after what happened yesterday, I wanted to make sure you were all right."

"Well, as you can see, I am." Keiko couldn't understand Shoji's reluctance to see his mother. She seemed like a wonderful person.

There was a strained silence in the room until Mr. Tochigi came in. Introductions had to be made all over again, and Keiko watched in surprise as her father became animated in his discussion with Mrs. Ibaragi. Of course it helped that she spoke fluent Japanese.

Shoji looked decidedly ill at ease, even tense.

"Shoji-san will make a fine husband for my daughter," Keiko's father told Mrs. Ibaragi, and the room grew uncomfortably quiet.

Without looking at her son, Mrs. Ibaragi, gently encouraged Keiko's father. "Do go on, Tochigi-san. You were saying?"

Shoji rose to his feet intent on intervening. A hand sliced his way by his mother had the effect of bringing him to silence. Keiko was amazed.

When Mr. Tochigi finished extolling the virtues of both his

daughter and future son-in-law, Mrs. Ibaragi turned an icy glare on her son.

"Well, I really must be leaving. I have to get back to town before dark. I'm staying at a hotel there." She fixed her son with an eloquent look. "Why don't you accompany me and see me situated?"

Keiko's father hastily agreed. "That is a good idea, Shoji-san. Take your time."

Keiko saw a swift glance at his mother tell Shoji that that was exactly what he was going to do.

After they left, Keiko exchanged a look with her brother.

"David! Can you imagine? Why would he want to be called Shoji?"

Keiko shrugged, going to the screen door and looking down the road. Either name sounded fine to her, but she thought she preferred Shoji. He looked more like a Shoji than a David to her.

&

As Keiko was washing the supper dishes, she could hear a car barreling down the road to their house. She grinned. Shoji must be in one fine temper.

But it wasn't Shoji that pulled into her drive. It was Cindy Masters, a friend from school. Surprised, Keiko went out to meet her on the porch.

"Cindy, what are you doing way out here this late?" she asked in surprise.

Cindy's face was filled with panic. "I have to see Kenji. Is he here?"

Frowning, Keiko nodded, pushing open the screen door. "Come in."

She shook her head quickly. "I can't. If I could just see Kenji?"

"Just a moment, I'll get him."

Keiko followed Kenji down the stairs and out onto the porch, where Cindy was still waiting. She twisted her driving gloves anxiously as she paced up and down. Turning in relief, she smiled at Kenji.

"Oh, Kenji. Am I glad I found you at home!"

"What's going on, Cindy?" Kenji frowned at the girl, and Keiko found herself holding her breath, waiting for the girl's explanation.

"You don't have a telephone, so no one could reach you. Mr. Shimura was taken away by the FBI."

The color drained from Kenji's face. "When?"

"Just this evening," she told him, twisting her hands together. "Mrs. Shimura wanted me to let you know."

"Has anyone contacted Sumiko?"

The other girl nodded. "She's getting ready to come home now. She plans to take the train and she'll be here by morning."

Kenji was already headed out the door. "Since Shoji has my car, I'm taking the truck."

Keiko nodded. "What are you going to do?"

"Someone needs to be with Mrs. Shimura. I don't know when I'll be back."

"Be careful."

Cindy followed him down the stairs. "I can't stay, either." She turned back to Keiko. "They're picking up Japanese men all over the place. I'm sorry, Keiko."

"Thank you, Cindy." Keiko hurried back inside. What about her own father? Would they come for him, too? Suddenly, she wished Shoji were here.

❧

Shoji twisted his face into a wry grimace as his mother's tirade continued. Rolling his eyes to the ceiling, he clenched his hands at his sides. Well, at least he knew one thing for certain. His mother had known nothing of his marriage contract.

"I can't believe you're going to go through with this!"

"Mother," he told her softly. "It was Father's last wish."

She stared at him in surprise. "I don't believe it. And besides, I could care less. An arranged marriage, of all things."

She threw herself into the overstuffed chair of the penthouse suite. "David, this is quite impossible."

Before he had gone to Japan, he and his mother had had a very close relationship. Now Shoji felt himself holding back from her. Was it because he was no longer a boy? Or was it because of his Japanese teaching? He found it hard to reconcile the way he was taught with the value system in America.

"Mother, I know this is hard for you to understand, but I intend to fulfill this contract."

"We'll get a lawyer."

"I don't want a lawyer." The cold anger in his voice brought his mother to silence. She watched him warily.

"Mother, this is a matter of honor."

"Honor, my foot." His darkening look only increased her own anger. "How can you stand there and calmly agree to such an arrangement? Of all the preposterous ideas!"

Shoji sighed heavily. "It's not a preposterous idea. It was Father's last wish."

"How do you know that? Who told you such a thing?"

"He did." The poignant tremor in his voice stilled her. There was no denying the truth of the statement.

"When?"

"When he was dying. I came to see him because he asked me to."

The color drained from her face. "You came to see your father and you didn't come to see me?"

He looked away. "I couldn't. I knew what you would say."

"You mean to tell me you are seriously considering marriage to a girl you hardly know?"

A soft look entered his eyes, bringing her up short. "I know her. She is not beautiful like the *geisha*. Even among the Japanese she would be considered ordinary to look at, but for her eyes."

His own eyes seemed to burn with a strange intensity.

"Whereas the other Japanese girls I know have such calm, vacant eyes, Keiko's glow with a mysterious inner fire. As though she has hidden depths and secrets it would take an eternity to unravel."

Mrs. Ibaragi's eyes went wide at her son's uncharacteristic eloquence. A sudden glow entered their depths as she stared at her son, a slow smile spreading across her face.

There was nothing to worry about where Shoji's marriage was concerned, she decided. Nothing at all.

❧

Keiko paced the floor. She was a nervous wreck. Where were Shoji and Kenji? It had been hours since Cindy had come and gone.

"Keiko-chan, come and read to me."

Keiko knew that her father was only trying to ease her mind, but she was afraid nothing would help. Sighing, she decided that reading the Bible couldn't hurt, either.

Flipping through the pages, she came to the account in John, chapter seventeen, where Jesus was praying in the garden. Her father's eyes were soft with sympathy as she read His petition for all believers, those at that time, and those to come. In verse twenty her mother had erased the words "them also" and replaced it with her own name, Yuki Tochigi.

Going back, she reread the verse again, inserting her own name. Such peace filled her as the realization came to her that Jesus had prayed for her long before she was ever born. She closed her eyes, imagining him in the garden talking to their Father on her behalf. He seemed to say, *I know what you are going to go through, Keiko, and I am here with you. If I am with you now, I will be with you then.*

"Keiko-chan." Her father's soft voice ended her peaceful reflections. "Read it now with my name."

Keiko gladly complied, and she saw the tears come to her father's eyes. "This Jesus was a remarkable man."

"Hai. Very remarkable."

A car coming down the drive sent Keiko scurrying to the door. In the dusky twilight she could just make out the form of the roadster. Shoji.

He came into the house, his look going from one to the other. "What's wrong?"

"Sumiko's father was picked up by the FBI."

His eyes narrowed. "When?"

"This evening."

He studied her thoughtfully before going to the living room and seating himself beside Mr. Tochigi. He tucked his lips together, watching Keiko as she slowly seated herself.

"Tochigi-san," he began. "I think it is time for Keiko and I to be married."

six

Keiko turned over in her bed, thumping her pillow angrily. Of all the nerve! Shoji had merely marched in and stated his demands.

Keiko gritted her teeth. To be fair, that was not totally accurate. He and Papa-san had sat for a long time discussing things while Keiko sat silently seething.

She didn't dare defy them right now. Her father's health was still too fragile to consider an open confrontation. Biting her lip, she rolled onto her back, covering her eyes with one arm.

How could Shoji even consider such a thing right now? Out of the clear blue sky! What was he thinking?

She heard the truck returning and hurriedly climbed out of bed, throwing on a flannel robe as she quickly went down the stairs. She stopped when she heard Kenji's angry voice.

"Someone told the authorities that Mr. Shimura was dealing with enemy agents overseas."

"I'll give you one guess who it was."

There was silence for several seconds before Kenji answered. "John Parker."

Keiko gasped. Surely even John Parker wouldn't do something so despicable. And even if he had, surely the authorities wouldn't believe him.

Eyes swiftly scanning the living room, Keiko soon realized that her father must have retired for the night. She sighed with relief. This was one more thing he didn't need to worry about.

Unsure why she did so, Keiko remained out of sight of the two young men. She felt slightly guilty for eavesdropping, but she couldn't help herself. It was the only way she knew of to find out what was truly going on. Both Shoji and Kenji seemed to think she needed to be protected from all the madness going on around them.

"What are you going to do?" Shoji asked.

Keiko could see her brother's face pinched with concern. His shoulders sagged with weariness.

"I came back to pick up a few things for the night, then I'll go back and stay with Mrs. Shimura. Sumiko will arrive some time in the morning and I'll pick her up at the train station. But I'm worried about Papa-san."

Shoji heaved a sigh. "Don't worry about things here. I'll take care of everything until you get back."

Keiko heard Kenji moving across the room and she hastily scrambled around the corner into the kitchen. She leaned back against the door, listening as Kenji mounted the stairs. Straining her ears, she listened for some sound to indicate Shoji's whereabouts. What was he doing anyway?

"You can come out now."

She jumped slightly at the whispered voice from the other side of the door. Feeling like a child caught with her hand in the cookie jar, Keiko slowly pushed open the door.

Shoji took in her embarrassed face, a small smile tilting the corners of his mouth.

"How did you know I was there?"

He grinned fully. "Keiko-chan, I could find you anywhere. You have a soft scent that is purely your own. Besides, I heard you."

Not sure whether to be offended or pleased, she settled for not commenting. Biting her lip, she glanced up the stairs.

"I hope he will be all right."

"Kenji can take care of himself." He silently stared at her, his look serious. "We need to try to keep as much as we can from your father. You agree?"

When she turned her look on him, there was fire in her

eyes. "As long as you don't do the same to me."

He pursed his lips, returning her look full force. "Agreed. Keiko. . ."

She was almost sure she knew what he was about to say.

"I'm tired. I'll see you in the morning."

He let her go, watching her make her way back up the stairs. When Keiko reached her door, she knew he was still watching her.

❧

They didn't hear from Kenji for three days. Keiko was frantic with worry, but she tried to hide it from her father. She busied herself around the house as much as possible.

Friday morning they heard Kenji's car, its roar unmistakable. Keiko flew out to the porch to meet him, her eyes going wide when she saw Sumiko sitting beside him.

Keiko had never seen her friend anything other than immaculate. The dispirited, disheveled girl who climbed from the car barely resembled the girl Keiko had always known. Sumiko's tired face was devoid of makeup, but that did nothing to detract from her beauty. If anything, she looked lovelier than before.

Sumiko had tied a kerchief around her head, knotting it at the back. Her dress was still the epitome of fashion, though, causing Keiko's lips to quirk slightly.

Running down the steps, Keiko took her friend into her arms.

"Oh, Sue. I'm so sorry. Have you heard anything?" Her eyes went to her brother.

He sighed heavily. "We just heard last night. They've taken Mr. Shimura to Missoula, Montana."

Keiko was surprised, to say the least. "Montana! Whatever for?"

Kenji went to Sumiko, placing a gentle arm around her waist. "Let's go inside, Kay. Sue needs to sit down."

"Of course. I'm sorry, I should have thought."

After Kenji had helped Sumiko into a chair, he turned to Keiko. "Where's Shoji? I need to talk to him."

"He's out in the field digging up rocks."

Keiko knew her brother was keeping something from her, but she wasn't sure what. Hopefully, Shoji would share whatever Kenji had to say.

"Would you like some tea, Sue?" she asked absently, her look following her brother out the door.

"Please. I need something to calm my nerves."

Keiko brought the tea from the kitchen, setting the tray on the table beside Sumiko.

"What's going on, Sue? How long are they going to keep your father?"

Burying her face in her hands, Sumiko burst into tears. "We don't know. They won't tell us anything, except that he and some others are being held for questioning."

Keiko knelt in front of her, taking Sumiko's cold, trembling hands into her own. She didn't know what to say, so she offered silent sympathy.

"This is all so crazy," the distraught girl continued. "My father has always been a loyal American. He loves this country. He wouldn't do anything to harm it."

"I know, Sue. And they'll realize it, too. We just have to have patience."

Sumiko snorted. "Not one of my strong suits."

Keiko grinned. "Mine either."

By the time the men returned, Sumiko had managed to gain control. Her face was still tight with worry and Keiko noticed that she clung to Kenji.

"I'm going to be staying with Sue and her mother for awhile," Kenji told them.

"But what about us? What about Papa-san?"

His eyes found Shoji's and Keiko noticed the look they exchanged. "Shoji is here. If I'm needed, you know where to reach me."

"Kenji," Keiko placed a hand on his arm to detain him. "Why did you take so long to tell us?"

His lips pressed into a tight line. "The FBI wouldn't let any of us leave Mrs. Shimura's house. An agent stayed the whole time to make sure no one came in or went out."

"He even answered our phone and refused to accept any calls," Sumiko stated heatedly.

"Why did they let you in?"

"I told them I was Sumiko's fiancé. I think they knew that they couldn't keep me out without trouble. Regardless of his actions, the agent seemed friendly enough."

Keiko watched them leave, a horrible feeling in the pit of her stomach. What next? Would they come for her father, too? If John Parker had been instrumental in causing Sumiko's father to be taken, wouldn't he have a much bigger grudge against Shoji and Kenji? This waiting was killing her.

Shoji curled his hands around her shoulders, pulling her back against his chest. His voice came softly against her cheek, stirring the strands of her long, dark hair that she had left hanging.

"It will be all right, Keiko. Everything will be all right."

But in the end, it wasn't. Anti-Japanese sentiment was growing every day. Even the Chinese consul had gone so far as to make the Chinese wear special badges to differentiate between them and the Japanese. Keiko felt as though the world were spinning out of control. How much longer could this go on?

❧

January first arrived, cold and unusually wet. Keiko shivered as she prepared the vegetables for the *ozoni,* a thick chicken stew made with carrots, bamboo sprouts, daikon, and taro roots. Kenji hated the dish, but since he would not be here, Keiko prepared it anyway, knowing her father would be pleased.

Every year it was the same thing. Papa-san was determined

to celebrate New Year's in the traditional Japanese way. First Keiko would fix his favorite buckwheat pancakes for breakfast, then Papa-san would pay off all his creditors, then came the traditional Japanese supper of *ozoni* and *mochi,* little rice dumplings served with the stew.

Fortunately for Keiko, Papa-san restricted his observance of the holiday to only the one day. She rolled her tired shoulders, closing her eyes against her tiredness. She had been busily cleaning the house from top to bottom, another Japanese custom for New Year.

Actually she hadn't minded all the extra work. It had helped to keep her mind off other things. Kenji came by from time to time, usually bringing Sumiko with him. One day he brought Mrs. Shimura and called a family conference.

In the end, it had been agreed upon by both parents that it would be all right for Kenji and Sumiko to marry. Keiko was surprised, but there was little she could do about it. Besides, she had always wished for Sumiko to be her sister. She just wished it could have been under more joyful circumstances.

Her eyes found Shoji's, and she could read his unspoken message. Although he had refrained from saying anything since the night he had talked to her father, Keiko knew that he was biding his time. It unnerved her.

When Shoji asked Keiko to go into town with him, Keiko agreed, mainly because her father had asked her to pay their creditors, the usual Japanese practice on New Year's.

They drove several miles in silence. Finally Shoji glanced at her briefly, his eyes typically inscrutable.

"How do you feel about Kenji and Sumiko?"

She squirmed on her seat. Surely he wouldn't bring up the subject of their marriage now.

"I'm pleased. I only wish it could be during a happier time."

Shoji sighed heavily, as though preparing himself for a big battle. "Keiko, Kenji tells me that the government is talking about moving the Japanese out of California."

"What?"

His eyes roved her surprised face before returning to the road. He nodded. "It's probably true. There is so much jealousy here by the *hakujin* who own the land that they will probably afford themselves of this opportunity to get rid of the 'yellow peril'."

Keiko grinned at his Japanese term for white people. If the situation were not so serious, she would have laughed.

He glanced at her, noting her amusement. "They are talking about sending all Japanese back to Japan, including American citizens."

"You can't be serious! I've never been to Japan in my life. I have no desire to go to Japan!"

He cocked a brow at her. "You needn't get so irate. It's a beautiful country."

She was appalled. "Are you seriously suggesting that I consider it?"

Shoji shook his head, his eyes going back to the road. "No. What I'm suggesting is that with everything that is happening, it's entirely possible that families and friends will become separated. I can't allow that. You're going to have to accept the fact that we need to be married soon."

She opened her mouth to protest, but his look silenced her. "Kenji has already realized this," he told her.

Keiko curled down into her seat to think about what he had just said. If Kenji was separated from Papa-san and her, what would become of them? Especially with Papa-san's delicate health.

She looked at Shoji, his attention focused on the road. He would stay with them, she was sure. She hadn't realized just how much she had come to depend on him over the last several months. But was dependency enough reason to get married?

She turned back to the view from the truck's window. At least he shared her faith in the Lord.

Shoji dropped her off at Mr. Anson's store.

"I'll park in front of the telegraph office," he told her. "I want to send a message to my mother, then I need to pick up some things from the hardware store. I'll meet you there."

Nodding her head in agreement, she climbed from the truck. When she went inside, she wasn't sure what to expect. She hadn't been to town since the bombing of Pearl Harbor. All she knew was that anti-Japanese sentiment was growing everywhere. She was more than a little frightened.

"Keiko! How nice to see you." Mr. Anson's cheerful voice caused her to relax. Mr. Anson had been a friend of the family for many years, and it seemed he hadn't changed.

"Come to pay your bill?"

Keiko grinned, shrugging her shoulders. "It is January first."

He laughed. "I know. I've been expecting you. I have it all made out."

He pulled the register from under the counter, pulling out a slip of paper. He handed it to Keiko and she smiled at the bold red words stamped across it. PAID IN FULL.

Keiko smiled when she handed him the money. "Thanks, Mr. Anson."

"Any time. How's your father, by the way?"

"He's doing better, but we still have to be careful with him."

"Well, you tell him I said 'hello,' okay?"

"I will."

Turning, Keiko left the store, stopping a moment to admire a pale blue dress that was hanging in the shop window next door. Keiko had never been able to afford purchasing a garment from Mrs. Saxon, but she admired the woman's abilities. Although Keiko could sew, she couldn't match Mrs. Saxon, even though Mrs. Saxon had been the one to teach their Home Ec class sewing.

"Keiko! Hello."

Keiko smiled at the small gray-haired woman. "Hello, Mrs. Saxon. I was just admiring the blue dress in your window."

Mrs. Saxon glanced at the garment mentioned. "It is pretty, isn't it? It's a new fabric from Paris."

They chatted for a few minutes before Keiko went on her way. As she was passing the alley next to the telegraph office, someone reached out a hand, snatching her into the darkened void.

Keiko opened her mouth to scream, but a hand shoved hard against her mouth. She was effectively pinned against the wall, and John Parker's angry eyes glittered menacingly down at her.

"Hello, *geisha* girl," he whispered, and Keiko flinched at his breath, so close to her face, reeking of alcohol.

Glancing from the sides of her eyes, she saw Mark Jeffries watching the street in case anyone came by. On her other side she found Stan Marcus leaning against the wall, his malicious grin sending shivers of apprehension sliding down her spine.

John moved his face in closer and Keiko tried to turn her face aside. It was no use. He was much too strong for her.

He uncovered her mouth long enough to replace his hand with his lips. She tried to squirm free, but this only seemed to incense him further. His teeth scraped against her lip, cutting it slightly, his fingers bruising her arms.

When he finally released her lips, his hand shot up to once again cover her mouth.

"I have a message for your boyfriend," he whispered. "Tell him I'm waiting for him. You give him the message, hear? But just to be sure."

Keiko heard a rip and felt the sleeve of her blouse give way. Her eyes widened in alarm, and she began to squirm in earnest.

"Remember, *geisha* girl. It's your word against mine. Just give your boyfriend the message."

He shoved her slightly toward the entrance to the alley, and she stumbled, clinging to the wall. Her legs were like jelly beneath her, but she managed to make it to the truck and crawled inside. Her body was shaking all over and tears ran in rivulets down her cheeks. She brushed them away with an impatient hand.

Inspecting the damage to her blouse, she was relieved that it was the right sleeve. At least she could keep it away from Shoji's sight. She knew she would never tell him. She couldn't. Not with the volatile temper he had.

When Shoji returned to the truck, Keiko continued to stare out the side window not really seeing anything. One hand clutched her blouse at the shoulder as she tried to make it seem as if nothing was out of the ordinary.

Shoji did nothing toward starting the vehicle and Keiko realized he sensed something was wrong.

"Keiko?"

Keiko bit hard into her bottom lip to keep from sobbing out loud. She felt Shoji move closer in the seat.

"Keiko, what's wrong?"

She felt his hands on her shoulders as he turned her toward him. A confused frown puckered his brows as his eyes roved over her face searching for some clue to her unusual behavior.

Her blouse fell apart under his fingers and his eyes went wide. His gaze rested on her lips, where a trickle of blood ran down the side. His face became like granite, his eyes glittering dangerously. "Who did this to you?"

Keiko tried to turn her face away, but he pulled her back, his fingers unusually gentle against her chin.

"Keiko." The hard, determined voice demanded an answer.

"Let it go," she told him softly, her voice wobbling with the effort.

Without him realizing it, Shoji's fingers bit into her chin. When she flinched, he jerked his hands away, clenching them on the steering wheel. He knew that Keiko had a stubborn streak a mile wide, and if she had decided not to tell him, he doubted there was anything he could do to make her.

Rage bubbled inside him unlike anything he had ever known before. He felt he could easily kill someone. *If any man hates his brother, he has committed murder already in his thoughts.*

Frustrated, he glared at Keiko. She watched him warily, gnawing on her bottom lip. The blood was still there. Grinding his teeth together, he looked away from her out the back window of the truck.

When he saw John Parker leaning nonchalantly against the telegraph office, a cigarette dangling from his mouth, he thought he had his answer. When John crossed one foot over the other, tipping him a one fingered salute, he was sure of it. His two buddies flanked him on either side.

Keiko followed his gaze, her eyes flying back to Shoji's face. She opened her mouth to protest, but it died on her lips at the look on his face.

Keiko laid a hand on his arm and felt the tenseness of his muscles beneath her fingers. His body was shaking with a violent rage that terrified her.

When he looked at her, Keiko felt her own body start to tremble. This must be what it was like to look death in the face. There was that about Shoji that told her he was beyond control and that someone was going to pay dearly.

When he spun to the edge of the seat reaching for the door, Keiko grabbed his black turtleneck sweater, clinging tightly with both hands.

"Shoji, no!"

He tried to shake her off, but she clung more tenaciously.

"No, Shoji!" she begged. "Please. He didn't do anything!"

Tears were once more streaming down her face.

"Listen to me! He didn't do anything. Nothing happened. Don't you see? If you hurt him, they'll put you in jail. They'll say you're a murdering Jap, and they'll kill you." She shook him to make him see reason. "Please, Shoji. Papa-san needs you. I need you!"

She felt his body go still, his look returning to her face. Some of the anger began to drain from him, but Keiko could tell that it wouldn't take much to fan it to life.

His fingers gently cupped her cheek, his thumb sliding softly across her lips. He bent, kissing the corner of her mouth where the blood had congealed on her cut.

Without looking around, he started the truck. Shifting into gear, he peeled out, leaving a burning black mark on the pavement. He never even looked around, but Keiko did.

There stood John Parker, his fists clenching and unclenching at his sides.

seven

Keiko stood on the porch of her home, gazing at the fields around her. Already there were signs of spring. Everything looked the same, yet everything was different.

When she saw a car in the distance, she thought it might be Kenji and Sumiko, but she soon realized that the gray sedan was not her brother. When the car pulled to a stop, Keiko's face grew grim. Mr. Dalrimple. What could he possibly want with them?

Mr. Dalrimple's burly form emerged from the car, a feigned smile upon his lips.

"Keiko! How are you?"

"I'm fine, Mr. Dalrimple. Is there something you wanted to see us about?"

The cigar that hung from the side of his mouth suddenly switched to the other side. "Well, yeah, but it's your father I need to see."

Keiko felt her heart drop. "He's inside. Come with me, please."

Keiko opened the door and led him inside to the living room. Her father was dozing in his favorite chair and she was reluctant to disturb him. Before she had the chance, he opened his birdlike eyes and stared up at them. Rising to his feet, he bowed low before Mr. Dalrimple.

"Dalrimple-san, how are you?"

The big man seemed slightly uncomfortable. "I'm, uh, fine, Tochigi-san. But I'm afraid I have some bad news for you."

Keiko moved to her father's side, unconsciously offering him her support.

"Please, sit down," her father offered.

Mr. Dalrimple glanced around him, shifting uncomfortably from one foot to the other. "No. I can't stay. I just wanted to let you know that this land has been sold."

Keiko's eyes widened. "You can't do that! This is our land! We bought it!"

Mr. Dalrimple snickered nervously. "Not technically. Technically it's my land."

Keiko felt rage rise like bile in her throat. "We gave you the money to purchase it for us! You didn't buy this land. You didn't sweat over it!"

"Keiko-san!"

Keiko glared at her father. "He can't do this!"

The cigar switched to the other side of the mouth. "Look, girlie, legally I can. I'm letting you know right now that you can stay here until the sale is final, but then you gotta go."

Keiko's father dropped into his chair, his face pinched white. Keiko flew to his side, dropping to her knees beside him. She glared up at the man standing beside her, so confidently sure of having his way.

"Get out!"

"Now look here."

"You heard the lady. Get out."

Mr. Dalrimple turned at Shoji's quiet voice. "Who're you?"

Keiko rose to her feet. "He's my fiancé. Now get out. I don't know what I can do legally, but I'll find something."

After Mr. Dalrimple was gone, Papa-san rose to his feet. "I think I would like to lie down for a bit."

Keiko searched his face worriedly, noting his unusual pallor. Her worried eyes found Shoji's.

"That's a good idea, Tochigi-san. We'll call you when supper is ready," Shoji told him.

As he walked slowly from the room, Keiko noticed how old he looked. She looked back at Shoji, who was studying her intently. She hadn't spoken to him much since the occurrence with John Parker several weeks ago.

"I have to go into town for awhile," he told her and Keiko panicked.

"I don't think that's a good idea."

His eyebrows rose to his forehead and Keiko gritted her teeth at his arrogant look. "I won't be long. But I need to talk to Papa-san for a minute before I leave."

"Let me go with you."

"And Tochigi-san?"

Keiko slumped onto the couch. She couldn't leave her father. Not now.

"Promise me you won't fight with John Parker."

His lip curled up at the corner. "I will not fight with John Parker if he will not fight with me."

With that she had to be satisfied. Moments later he left the house.

❧

When Shoji returned, Kenji was following him. Sumiko was with Kenji along with Mrs. Shimura. Behind them another car pulled to a stop and Mr. Kosugi, the minister climbed out.

Surprised, Keiko invited everyone inside.

"Well, Keiko," Mr. Kosugi smiled. "After watching you grow up and baptizing you so many years ago, I now get to marry you."

His grin went from ear to ear. Kenji was studying Keiko seriously. He laid a hand on her shoulder.

"I'm happy for you, Sis. I don't think you could find a finer man."

Sumiko grinned at her. "You sly old dog. Imagine not telling your best friend."

Keiko couldn't say anything. Her throat was dry, and she was too stunned to do more than nod her head at everyone's congratulations.

Shoji followed her father as he entered the room. Her father bowed low before Mr. Kosugi.

Mr. Kosugi returned his bow deferentially. "Tochigi-san,

you must be very happy for your daughter."

Her father bowed again. "I am. Shoji will make a fine son."

Keiko moved as though in a dream. Mr. Kosugi performed the typical American wedding ceremony, his droning voice lulling Keiko into an apathetic acceptance of everything that was happening. Papa-san seemed to accept the ceremony, even though it was not a traditional Japanese one. Keiko had to be thankful for that at least.

When Shoji's lips closed over hers in the conventional sealing of the vows, Keiko found her knees buckling beneath her. Shoji supported her with his arms, but there was no disguising the fear in her eyes. She had just agreed to live with this man for the rest of her life. She didn't know much about him, and what little she did know frightened her half to death.

No, that wasn't exactly true. She knew he could be extremely gentle and kind, and for the most part he was. It was only when the demons of his past came back to haunt him that she was afraid. His inscrutable almond eyes stared down into hers, and she felt some of her fears subside.

Later, Keiko sat in the garden next to the pool, trailing her fingers in the water. Her unfocused gaze rested on the koi fish darting to and fro. She didn't hear Shoji come up behind her and jumped when he sat down next to her.

They were quiet for a long time, neither knowing what to say. Finally, Keiko turned to face him.

"What kind of marriage do you want?"

He didn't pretend to misunderstand her. Taking one of her hands into his, he began to stroke it tenderly without looking her in the face.

"I want a real marriage."

Only then did his eyes come back to hers. There was a softness in his eyes she had never seen before. When he leaned forward, she didn't draw back. When his lips touched hers tentatively, she kissed him back. She still didn't know how she felt about him, but she knew he attracted her and now they were husband and wife.

He deepened the kiss, pulling her fully into his embrace. When he lifted his head, there was a glow in his eyes that was more intense than anything she had ever seen before. Her heart began to hammer furiously in her chest.

"Let's go to bed," he told her quietly, lifting her gently into his arms and carrying her inside.

❧

Three days later Kenji returned. His set face let Keiko and Shoji know something was wrong. Fortunately for them, Papa-san was taking a nap.

"There's nothing we can do about the land," he told them without preamble. "The same story is being played over and over all over California and other states besides."

Keiko sighed. "What now?"

"That's the least of our worries," he told them. "Word just came down that President Roosevelt has issued Executive Order 9066."

"What does that mean?" Keiko asked, fearful of the answer.

"It means that the president has just given the government the authority to declare the Japanese in this country 'hostile aliens'."

"Even us?"

Kenji shook his head. "Not yet, though we're to be treated as such. There's word coming down that the Japanese are going to be sent to internment camps."

Keiko sat down on the steps. "Dear Lord, how can You let this happen?"

"Mass evacuations are about to begin. I came to tell you that, and to invite you to Sumiko's and my wedding."

Keiko was stunned, though she knew she shouldn't have been. Shoji was pleased, pumping Kenji's hand up and down.

"When?" he wanted to know.

"Tomorrow morning at ten o'clock at the Japanese Community Church. You'll come?"

"Nothing could keep us away," Keiko remonstrated.

"I'll let you tell Papa-san. I gotta get back."

Shoji placed an arm around Keiko's waist and they watched Kenji disappear from sight. Three days of being married, and she still wasn't accustomed to his touch. Would she ever be? Could she truly learn to love him someday, like her mother had her father?

Pulling away, she retreated to the safety of the house. She knew he wouldn't follow her, he had too much to do in the fields.

For some reason she was shy with him during the day. But at night. . . Her face crimsoned as she remembered the past three nights. Could she possibly respond to a man the way she did Shoji if she didn't care? It was something to ponder.

❧

Sumiko's wedding was as unlike Keiko's as it could have been. There were flowers and candles everywhere. The church was decorated fully and Keiko wondered how Sumiko had managed to do it in such a short time.

"Kay!" Sumiko rushed forward grabbing Keiko by the hand. "Come on! I thought you'd never get here!"

"Why aren't you dressed?" Keiko demanded, her eyes going over Sumiko's plain house dress.

"I will, but I had to see that you got dressed first." Sumiko shoved her into one of the small classrooms. "Put that on."

Keiko's eyes widened at the beautiful blue dress that had been hanging in Mrs. Saxon's shop window. It completely took her breath away. Sumiko grinned, pleased with her surprise.

"Well, you didn't think I could have my matron of honor dressed in anything but the best, did you?"

Perplexed, Keiko could only stare at her friend. "But how did you manage this? They've frozen everyone's bank accounts. How did you get the money for all this?"

Sumiko giggled. "Daddy has a hidden safe in the house.

That's where he keeps a large portion of our money. He doesn't exactly trust banks."

Keiko knew that Mr. Shimura was a wealthy man, but she hadn't known exactly how wealthy.

"Hurry up, for goodness' sake." Sumiko quickly pulled her own dress from a mannequin in the corner. Keiko gasped at its beauty, the pearls on the bodice shimmering in the sunlight.

"Isn't it a pip?" Sumiko asked, her eyes dreamy. "Of course, Mrs. Saxon made it and anything she makes is bound to be beautiful."

When Keiko preceded Sumiko down the aisle, her throat was choked with tears. This was how a wedding should be. Beautiful flowers, a beautiful church, and a bride and groom whose eyes glowed when they looked at each other.

❧

When they went to bed that night, Shoji leaned over her, tracing a finger across her forehead. In the moonlight she could see his broad-shouldered physique. There was nothing about him that wasn't physically perfect.

"I'm sorry, Keiko-chan." His soft voice sent shivers of awareness tingling up her spine.

"For what?" she asked curiously.

"I know how much beautiful weddings mean to women. I would have done the same for you if I had had time."

Her eyes studied his and she could see that he was sincere.

"It's no matter," she told him, and suddenly realized that it wasn't. It wasn't the wedding, it was the marriage that counted. Her mother had given everything to her marriage, and her father had fallen hopelessly in love with her.

Keiko smiled as she thought of doing the same. She knew if she wasn't already in love with her husband she was halfway there. She remembered her mother telling her once, "Love is not a feeling, Keiko-chan. It is a decision."

Deciding right then and there that she would make this the

best marriage possible, Keiko tried to pull Shoji's lips down to hers. He held back, questioning with his eyes.

Keiko smiled softly, her eyes glowing, and whatever had been bothering Shoji must have been put to rest, for his lips met hers eagerly in the dark.

≈

By the middle of March, Lieutenant General John L. DeWitt was ready to execute President Roosevelt's executive order. He did it with such enthusiasm, no one was left in doubt as to his feelings for the Japanese.

Since early in March, a curfew had been imposed on Japanese Americans. No one was allowed on the streets past six o'clock and no one was allowed to travel more than five miles from their home.

This presented a problem for Keiko since she lived fifteen miles from town. Keiko fumed, wondering how the government expected them to arrange for supplies with no phone. Her dilemma was solved a few days later when she saw Mr. Anson's black truck coming toward their house.

He jumped out of the truck, and although there was a smile on his face, Keiko could sense his anger. She watched him go to the back of the truck and pull out a large cardboard box. Marching over to her, he demanded, "Where do you want this?"

Puzzled, she looked at Mr. Anson for some explanation.

He stared belligerently back at her. "This stupid government might keep you from coming to me, but they can't keep me from coming to you. You tell me if there's anything else you need, and I'll see that you get it."

"But. . .but I can't pay you. Our bank account has been frozen."

He waved his hands. "I know all that. It doesn't matter. You've always been a good customer and I know you'll pay when this crazy government comes to its senses and begins to treat you like human beings again."

Tears welled up in Keiko's eyes though she tried to prevent it. She knew Mr. Anson was already uncomfortable. His kindness and generosity were what made him such a special man, and she somehow knew that he wouldn't appreciate her profuse thanks.

Shoji appeared at her side, his eyes on the store owner.

"Mr. Anson has brought us some supplies," she told him.

Face red with embarrassment, Mr. Anson turned back to his truck. Reaching inside, he pulled out another box. "I told Keiko you can pay me back whenever."

Laying the box at Keiko's feet, Mr. Anson smiled. "You've done business with my store so long, I reckon I pretty much got it figured what you need. Oh, and congratulations on your marriage."

Glancing over the supplies, Keiko realized he was right.

"Thank you, Mr. Anson," she told him quietly, and the deferential tone of her voice conveyed her full meaning to him. She was very thankful, and she appreciated his kindness.

Relaxing, he grinned back at her. "I'll come out this way every Friday until this stupid restriction is lifted. You just let me know what you need."

Climbing back into his truck, he smiled at them both before turning and heading back the way he had just come.

"People like him more than make up for the people like John Parker," Shoji told her softly, his eyes still on the truck.

"Hai."

Shoji smiled at her, giving her a quick kiss on the lips. "I've still got work to do."

"Shoji?"

"Hai?" He halfway turned back to her.

"Why are you bothering with the field when it's no longer ours?"

He looked as if he was about to say something, when suddenly he shrugged his shoulders. "What would you suggest I do? Sit in the house all day?"

Knowing what a physical person he was, Keiko understood his problem. He could never just sit around and do nothing. She watched him go, a feeling of pride washing over her. She would never need to worry as long as she had Shoji.

The rest of the week, neighbors continually made a path to their door. All of them white, since it was beyond the five-mile limit of the other Japanese in the area.

Keiko didn't realize just how many friends they had. Her heart warmed with appreciation for them all. Everyone brought something with them.

Mrs. Ames brought her famous sourdough bread, Mrs. Simpson brought an apple pie, Mr. Pierce brought some tools he thought Shoji could use. Keiko watched her father become once more the man she remembered, and she knew that he was growing on love.

One night Keiko heard the front screen door open quietly while they were in bed. She was about to go and check it out when Shoji pinned her to the mattress.

"Stay here," he whispered, and she found that she had no desire to disobey him. He moved with such stealth that he was out of the room before she knew it.

A strangled cry brought her from her bed, sending her flying down the stairs. Funny, she had no fear for Shoji, but she could just picture John Parker lying on the floor in a pool of his own blood. There was no doubt in her mind that Shoji could be lethal if he needed to be.

Flicking on the light, she stood on the bottom stair. Her brother dangled from Shoji's hands. Keiko covered her mouth to keep from laughing at the surprised expression on her brother's face, then realized that something must be terribly wrong for Kenji to break the curfew. The smile fell from her face and she rushed to his side.

Shoji was already apologizing, but Kenji brushed his concern aside, straightening the collar on his shirt. "It's okay, it's okay! I'm thankful my sister and father are so well protected.

But, couldn't you give a guy some notice?"

Keiko grabbed his arm. "What's wrong? Why are you here?"

They all sat down in the living room and Kenji leaned forward, his face serious. "I don't know if you've heard yet, but they've begun the mass evacuation. They started at Terminal Island today after giving the people just three days' notice."

Shoji sucked in his breath. "It's finally come."

"I came to tell you so that you can be prepared. They're only allowing people to take what they can carry."

Shoji sat with his elbow draped on the arm of the chair, his lips pushed between his thumb and forefinger. He was so silent Kenji shifted uncomfortably.

"I can't stay any longer. I have to get back."

"How did you get here?" Keiko asked. "I didn't hear your car."

"I didn't want to chance using it. The noise would give me away. I walked."

"You walked?" Keiko's voice rose a full octave.

Remembering his own sojourn, Shoji grinned. "It can be done."

Shoji pulled Keiko to her feet and they walked with Kenji to the door.

"Be careful, Kenji!" Keiko implored her brother.

Kenji smiled at his sister before shaking hands with Shoji. "Take care of our girl."

"I will."

Keiko watched her brother's form swallowed up by the darkness, a lump forming in her throat. Shoji wrapped his arms around her from behind.

"He'll be okay," he told her, his voice husky against her ear.

Nodding, she said nothing.

"Come back to bed."

Keiko followed him up the stairs, her heart aching for what

was happening to them all. Never had she felt so victimized, not even when John Parker had assaulted her. She could understand his hatred. But the whole country?

Remembering her path of visitors, she shook her head. No, not the whole country.

She curled into Shoji's arms, knowing that come what may, she would be safe with her husband and her Lord. With both of them looking out for her, she knew she had nothing to fear. But deep down inside, there was still that little niggle of worry.

Keiko stood at the sink washing dishes the next morning when it occurred to her that it had been a little over a year since Shoji had first come into their lives. Sadly, she had missed putting out her dolls for *Hinamatsuri*, but Shoji had felt it best that they remain packed away just in case they received notification to evacuate.

Keiko still had a hard time believing it could actually happen. It was appalling to believe that their government could so haphazardly disregard the Constitution's protection of its citizens.

So much had changed in just a year, not the least of which she was now Shoji's wife. Had anyone told her a year ago that this would be so, she would have laughed in their face. But then, had anyone told her that she would be forced to leave her home just because she was Japanese, she would have scorned that, also.

When she heard a car coming down the road, she hastily wiped her hands on the kitchen towel and went to the front door. She didn't recognize the man who stepped from the car. His black coat reached to his feet and she could see a black pinstriped suit underneath.

He removed his hat, creasing the gray felt brim between his fingers. "I'm looking for a Mr. Tochigi or a Mr. Ibaragi."

He turned as Shoji came from the side of the house. As per usual, Keiko hadn't even heard him arrive.

"I'm Ibaragi," he told the man, and Keiko realized the inscrutable mask was hiding his anger. She was beginning to know her husband's moods.

The man handed Shoji a paper. Shoji glanced at it, his face going white.

"What is it?" Keiko asked him, coming to peer over his shoulder.

"Our evacuation orders," he told her, no inflection in his voice. He handed the paper to Keiko, his eyes focused on the man before him. "We have ten days to report to the Tulare Assembly Center."

"Ten days! But that's not enough time." Keiko directed an accusing glare at the man.

"I'm sorry, but it's all the time you have." He looked at Shoji. "The male head of each house needs to register. You need to report to the Civil Control Station being set up at the Japanese Community Church."

Placing his hat back on his head, he climbed back into his car and sped away.

Shoji stood staring after the man a long time. "Well, at least we know the restriction has been lifted."

A short while later, Keiko watched Shoji follow the same path as their visitor in her father's truck. Burying her face in her hands she tried to pray, but suddenly, she found she had nothing to say.

eight

There was an air of abandonment that surrounded the house, its insidious presence moving among the rooms as each was quickly emptied of its residents. The only furniture left in the house was the mattresses they still slept on and a small table in the corner of the living room that housed a lone occupant.

The small bonsai tree had resided in the same spot for as long as Keiko could remember living in this house. It had been given to her father the day he was born, and now fifty-six years later it was not much larger than when it had been given to him. Her father tended it lovingly, believing that if the tree died, he would also die.

The gentle sadness on his face caused her heart to constrict within her.

"What is troubling you, Papa-san?"

Startled, he turned quickly at her voice. His hands moved softly over the needles of the pine. He heaved a huge sigh.

"I cannot take my tree with me. We are allowed only what we can carry, and there are too many things we need for me to worry about my tree."

Shoji came in the door in time to hear his last words. Dropping the dusty suitcase he had retrieved from the storage shed, he went and laid a hand on the old man's shoulder.

"You carry the tree, Tochigi-san, and let me worry about the rest."

Keiko agreed, but her father was already shaking his head.

"No. I must do my part, also. We need to take many things with us, and there are only the three of us to do it."

"Mr. Anson has agreed to store our things for us," Keiko told him. "At least we don't need to worry about that."

92

Shoji nodded. "And your tree will go with us if I have to carry it in my teeth."

Keiko's heart swelled with appreciation. If anyone would understand her father's need for his tree, it was Shoji. She smiled warmly at him, her eyes glowing with her feelings.

Shoji turned away, checking over the bags Keiko had packed. He smiled slightly, realizing that she had packed sparingly, hoping to relieve him of some of the weight he would need to carry.

"Keiko, where is the hot plate?"

Looking down, her face filled with color as she realized he had figured out what she had tried to do. "I thought perhaps we would not need it since the government will provide us with meals."

Shoji went to the kitchen, returning with the aforementioned article in his hands. Shifting things in the duffel bag, he placed the hot plate inside.

"I think perhaps the government probably has a different idea of what constitutes a meal than you and I. Besides, Papa-san will want his tea."

"But Shoji, we already have too much to carry as it is."

"Keiko," he told her softly, "let me worry about carrying our bags, and you worry about making sure we have what we'll need."

Heaving a sigh of acquiescence, she turned to her father. "I still have some things I need to go through in my bedroom. Is there anything I can help you with?"

Her father shook his head. "Iie. You go do what you need to do."

Shoji found her an hour later sitting cross-legged in the middle of her bedroom. She glanced up as he came in, answering his unspoken question.

"Mementos," she told him, and her voice was thick with the tears she was trying hard to suppress.

He came and sat beside her, leaning forward to investigate

the small box she was digging in. Reaching in, he pulled out a dried arrangement of flowers twined together with a faded royal blue ribbon.

"Aren't these the flowers I gave you for the prom?"

Looking down at her lap, Keiko's cheeks filled with fiery color. "Hai."

When she dared a look at his face, she found him watching her, his brown almond eyes unfathomable. Frowning, she wondered what was going on behind that inscrutable mask now.

Gently, he placed the corsage back in the box. When his eyes again found her face, they were no longer mysterious but filled with a strange longing. Keiko sucked in a breath, not releasing it until he lifted one hand and softly stroked her cheek.

It had been eight days since Shoji had last touched her. Eight long days, and eight even longer nights. She leaned her cheek against his palm, smiling slightly.

For some reason he was tense. It communicated itself to her through his very touch. He seemed to be fighting a battle within himself, but for what reason she had no idea.

Growling softly, he leaned forward and kissed her. When she readily responded, he pulled her tightly into his embrace, taking her down to the floor beneath him.

Keiko wrapped her arms around his neck, trying to pull him further toward the vortex of emotions she was experiencing. When he suddenly pulled away, she was confused.

Shoji rose quickly to his feet, brushing a hand through his hair. His emotions were once again hidden behind his dark eyes, but Keiko knew that he had been just as affected as she by their encounter.

"Keep your mementos, Keiko. Perhaps they will remind you of a happier time."

Keiko watched him leave the room, more confused than ever. What made Shoji draw away from her? Was it possible that he held her partially accountable for the situation they were in? Did he resent her country for what it was doing to them?

Getting up, she went to the window and saw Shoji heading for his favorite spot in the garden. What would happen to that garden when they left? An aching sadness left her depressed. Nothing would ever be the same again. Shoji was right. She should keep her mementos because they might very well be the only thing she had left to remember of her life in this country.

Several hours later they were ready to leave. It had been decided that they would spend the night with Kenji and Sumiko tonight since they lived in town, thereby saving themselves the embarrassment of being picked up by an army truck in the morning.

Shoji checked the bags one more time to be sure they had their family identification number on them. They were no longer the Tochigi or Ibaragi family. Now they were Family 73896. That little ticket with that little number seemed such a betrayal of everything Keiko had been taught to believe as an American.

That the government could so forget itself as to call American citizens "non-aliens" and refuse them due process of law in the name of the "protection" of that government was more ludicrous than anything she had as yet experienced. The pain of that rejection was almost overwhelming.

They made the trip into town in silence, each busy with their own thoughts.

Keiko sat between her husband and father feeling lonelier than she had ever felt, even lonelier than when her mother had died. She had a father on one side of her, too frail in health to be worrying with her own morbid thoughts, and a husband on the other side of her that had suddenly become more of a stranger than when she had first married him.

Kenji was waiting for them when they pulled into the

Shimura driveway. The huge structure inspired the same feeling of wonder in Keiko that she had felt as a child. Mr. Shimura was a very wealthy man, and that was probably the very reason he found himself in Missoula, Montana. Many in the vicinity were jealous of Mr. Shimura's wealth.

Sumiko showed Keiko and Shoji to their room while Kenji showed Papa-san his. Mrs. Shimura was already in bed even though it was still very early in the evening.

"Mama had to be given tranquilizers," Sumiko told them. "It's more than she can take."

"What of your father?" Keiko asked her.

Turning away, Sumiko bit her lip. "We hear from him often by telegraph. I think he is more worried about us than we are about him." A tear dripped slowly down her cheek. "No, that's not true. He can't be any more worried than we are about him. We've heard that some of the men in Montana might be moved."

"Where?" Shoji asked.

Sumiko shrugged. "We don't know. Rumor has it that some are believed to be spies for Japan."

Keiko was filled with a righteous wrath. "That's the most ridiculous thing I've ever heard!"

"Is it?" Kenji walked up and put his arm around his wife. "We know that, but do you remember Mr. Ito?"

Keiko did. The man was positively Japanese through and through. They had always wondered why he had come to America in the first place when it was so obvious that Japan was the country that he loved.

"There are others like him, Keiko, and though they are probably as harmless as you or I, you can't blame the country for its doubts at a time like this."

"Can't I?" The angry sparkle in Keiko's eyes warned her brother that it was time to change the subject.

"We have to meet at the Japanese Community Church first thing in the morning. We better get some sleep."

That night Keiko lay in the still darkness listening to the even breathing of her husband. Again he had turned away from her as soon as they had climbed into bed. Was it something she had done? Was he tired of her already?

She curled into a small ball, biting the knuckles of her hand to stop the tears that threatened to come. Her quiet sniffles were muffled in the soft feather pillow that she clutched as though it were a lifeline.

With a groan Shoji rolled over, pulling Keiko roughly into his arms.

"Don't cry, Keiko-chan."

Instead of helping, the endearment made her cry all the harder. She burrowed against his shoulder, allowing the tears she had been holding back for days to work their healing balm on her scarred soul.

"Shhh. Don't cry, little one."

"I can't help it," she gulped. "Everything is gone. Everyone is gone!"

"That's not true, and you know it," Shoji admonished softly. "You still have Kenji, Papa-san, Sumiko, and I."

She looked up at his face in the dark. "What if they send Kenji somewhere else? What if they take Papa-san to Montana? What if you. . ." She stopped, unable to complete the thought.

"What if I what? They won't separate us, Keiko, you know that. We are both American citizens. Husband and wife. They won't separate us."

He sounded so sure of himself, yet hadn't he left her in a way already?

"Shoji, do you love me?"

She felt him stiffen against her. He started to pull away, but she clung to him.

"Answer me. Do you?"

He tried to pry her fingers loose from their grip against his shoulders. "Keiko, now is not the time to discuss this."

"Why? Why can't you just admit that the only reason you married me was for some honor-bound duty you felt justified in performing?"

He seemed as surprised at her anger as she was. Suddenly she let go of him and rolled to the edge of the bed. Before she could get up, Shoji pulled her back.

She could see his eyes glittering down at her in the moonlight. She could sense his anger and was suddenly afraid.

"Let me go," she commanded, but he ignored her.

"Are you suddenly unsure of my feelings for you because I no longer make love to you?"

Hot color flooded her cheeks. One thing about Shoji, he had an uncanny knack for reading her mind. She struggled again, embarrassed to even be having this conversation.

He shook her none too gently. "Listen to me. I will not have a child born into captivity like some animal at the zoo."

She stilled at his declaration, her eyes roving his features. The shadows gave him a grim, unsmiling appearance.

"I know that you aren't already with child." Again Keiko felt the hot color flood her cheeks. "And I intend to make sure it stays that way."

Releasing her, he rose to his feet. She could see his broad-shouldered silhouette in the moonlight that was slanting through the window and across the floor.

"Go to sleep, Keiko," he commanded harshly. She watched him pull on his clothes in preparation for leaving.

"Where are you going?"

The trepidation in her voice brought a long sigh from him. He crossed to her, sitting beside her on the bed.

"I have some things to do. Here. In the house. I'm not going outside, okay? Now go to sleep."

He pulled the covers gently up against her neck. Bending, he kissed her briefly on the lips. "I'm not sure what I feel right now. Things are all mixed up. In here." He pointed to his head. "But you can be sure of one thing. I will always be here for you. Understand?"

Keiko knew she would have to be satisfied with that for the time being. She could better understand his reasoning now. She had never thought about becoming pregnant. Instead of making her afraid, the thought warmed her.

But Shoji was right. Now was not the time. But someday. Someday.

❧

The sidewalks were crowded with the milling throngs of Japanese. Many Keiko recognized, but many she did not.

Everyone clung to their luggage, chattering to others around them. The church was offering them sandwiches and drinks, but most were too distraught to partake of the friendly repast.

Keiko watched a young mother of two struggling with her children. She was obviously very pregnant and very frazzled. Where was her husband?

As she watched, a young man hurried to her side. Taking the youngest child from her arms, he lifted a huge suitcase with one hand and told her to follow him.

Keiko jumped when Kenji dropped an arm across her shoulders. He smiled wryly down at her upturned face. "It's only me."

They watched the progress of the young couple together.

"The children, Kenji. What of the children? What harm could they possibly do?"

The smile left his face and he straightened his shoulders. "None, but do you think they would really want to be separated from their families?"

"I guess not." Keiko was thinking of their own upcoming separation. She had found out this morning that Kenji would be going to Tanforan Assembly Center while they would be going to Tulare. Only the United States government had any idea why.

Turning, Keiko hugged her brother tightly. His arms tightened around her and there was a suspicious huskiness in his voice when he finally managed to speak.

"Keiko, I don't know what's going to happen, but I want you to know that I thank God Shoji is here to take care of you."

She nodded into his chest without speaking. Already tears were pouring from her eyes and she had the distinct feeling it was going to be a long flowing river.

Shoji joined them, giving them time together just by being silent. Finally, Kenji handed Keiko over to her husband.

"I have to get back to Sumiko and Mrs. Shimura." His eyes found Shoji's and held. "Take care of them."

Shoji nodded briefly, sharing Kenji's pain. There was no doubt that Kenji loved his father and sister, and his brother-in-law, if Keiko read him right. It was all too evident in the repressed tears he fought to control. Shaking hands, the two men parted and Kenji strode away.

Struggling with her own tears, Keiko leaned back against Shoji when he curled his hands around her shoulders. Everywhere people were calling good-byes. Keiko soon realized that she wasn't the only one having a good cry.

Armed security guards roamed among the Japanese, their rifles loaded, their bayonets at the ready. Just their presence made Keiko go cold all over. Suddenly she felt like a woman without a country, like she had no place to call home.

"It's time to go," Shoji told her, turning her to where she knew her father was waiting.

He sat resolutely, guarding his precious bonsai tree. Keiko grinned through her tears. What a major battle that had been, but Keiko soon found out that steel had met tide when it came to the forces of will of her parent and husband. She was only now beginning to realize how inflexible such a soft person as her husband could be.

Slowly they made their way to the buses. Shoji carried the major load of luggage, but Keiko had insisted on doing her part. Between them they had convinced Papa-san that he would best serve their purpose if he could carry his tree and help navigate them through the crowd.

It seemed hours before the buses were finally ready to roll, not that Keiko was in any particular hurry.

Almost as though the Lord were feeling their sorrow, a gentle rain began to fall, turning suddenly into a torrent. The sun refused to show its face and Keiko blessed its seeming sensitivity. Surely the Lord was looking down on this atrocity and feeling her pain.

She knew without a doubt that most of her fellow passengers were either Buddhist or of the Shinto faith, but the Lord was with her.

Her father sat beside her, staring silently out the window. Keiko felt a pang of alarm. What would this do to her father's frail heart? To lose everything, including your only son. Almost as though he could read her thoughts, he turned to her.

"At least I have you, Keiko-chan, and Shoji."

Keiko turned to watch her husband, who was standing at the rear of the bus. Yes, at least they had Shoji. Strong, dependable Shoji.

When she studied her father's face closer, she could see the tired lines that radiated out from his eyes. Their dark amber-colored irises blinked back at Keiko sedately and she wondered at his calm.

Keiko felt the tears threatening again as she watched their little town slowly receding in the distance. Her home, gone. Her brother, gone. All her memories. No, they weren't gone. They could never be taken away. Would she ever see her home again?

She was surprised when her father took her hand into his own leathery one and began to absently stroke it. When he spoke, his voice seemed to come from far away.

"At least your mother was not here to see this."

Keiko gnawed on her bottom lip. "Do you think she knows what's happening to us? Do you think she can see us now?"

He turned surprised eyes to her. "Does not your Bible say that there are no tears in heaven?"

"Hai."

He turned back to the window. "Then she does not know what is happening, because she would surely be crying right now."

Keiko felt humbled. Here she had thought to comfort her father and instead he was trying to comfort her. Somehow his words were not as comforting as they should have been. She had always wanted to believe that her mother was watching over her, smiling with her triumphs, crying over her hurts.

She realized then that she had allowed her mother to take the place of God. He was the one who rejoiced with her victories and hurt when she hurt. He was the one who watched over her, took care of her. Even Shoji could not replace Him.

Bowing her head, she prayed silently as the miles rolled past. She gave herself into His care and turned her anger and bitterness over to Him to deal with. It wasn't the Americans or the Japanese that was the real enemy. It was Satan, and she realized how in control he was. But God was sovereign. Nothing could happen without His will. With that thought, peace descended.

The peace stayed with her even when she opened her eyes and saw the looming grandstands of Tulare. Dusk was falling and it was hard to see, but the darkness did nothing to hide the bleakness, the barrenness of their new home. The converted racetrack loomed ominously against the darkening sky.

Barbed wire fences gave Keiko the feeling that she was some horrible criminal. She felt a tightness in her chest. Is this what it felt like to walk through a prison door knowing you might never come back out?

Faces peered at them from the semi-darkness. Almond eyes searching for family and friends.

As the bus drove through the gates, Keiko heard them clang shut behind them. Shivering, she turned to find her husband's eyes watching her. The strength that flowed from him seemed to reach through the fog of her fear and she felt her peace restored.

God had sent her Shoji to be the arms that she needed to wrap securely around her in her most trying times. At first it had been her mother, then her father, and now, Shoji. His was the physical love she needed just as God was the spiritual.

They were unloaded from the bus and directed to an area where they filled out registration papers. Soldiers inspected their baggage for contraband items. Keiko felt her anger rise when one woman was relieved of her Japanese Bible, but she kept silent.

Everyone had to go through a cursory medical examination, and Keiko wondered what they would say about her father's heart condition. Did they realize they could very well be sentencing him to death?

Surprisingly, they said nothing, allowing Papa-san to pass through the inspection line. Shoji took their suitcases and prepared to leave. The rest of their luggage would be delivered later when the bus was unloaded.

Keiko followed her husband and father through ankle-deep mud to some buildings toward the rear of the center. She was so tired that all she wanted was a place to lay her head and go to sleep.

They stopped outside what appeared to be a stable, and Keiko wondered how much longer it would be before they reached their final destination.

"Well, this is it," Shoji told them. "C-5."

He opened a small door and went inside. Keiko blinked at his disappearing form. Surely he had to be kidding. This was a horse stable, for goodness' sake.

Suddenly a light illuminated the entryway. Shoji returned to the door, motioning them inside.

Keiko followed her father up the one step, stopping in the doorway. Her eyes went wide. In this ten foot by ten foot space, three army cots drooped lazily against the floor. An attempt had been made to whitewash the walls, but not before any insect species had been removed. Little white bodies clung to the walls.

Keiko could smell the still lingering smell of the horses that had so recently made their homes here. Other evidences of their occupation were the teeth marks in the stall doors and particles of straw that littered the floor.

Shoji stood watching her from below the one lone lightbulb that hung suspended from the center of the ceiling.

"Is this it?" she wanted to know.

His lips twisted crookedly. "I'm afraid so."

That was the last thing Keiko remembered before darkness descended.

nine

When Keiko slowly opened her eyes again, her mind was still foggy. She had been dreaming a wonderful dream where her mother was chasing her through a field of flowers, her long dark hair streaming out behind her. Picking a daisy from the millions around her, she handed it to her mother, whose radiant smile brought an answering response from Keiko.

"You are my little angel, Keiko-chan."

Keiko smiled her little girl smile, reaching up a hand to touch her mother's soft features. Suddenly the smile left her face.

"I am not your God, Keiko. Remember that. I love you, but I am not your God."

She took one of Keiko's hands into her own, stroking it softly. "Do you hear me, Keiko?"

"I hear you, Mama," she answered softly.

Slowly the image faded and the eyes peering down at her so intently were not her mother's. They had been replaced by eyes the color of mahogany, alive with worry.

"Keiko, can you hear me?"

Finally the scenery came into focus and Keiko found herself staring up into Shoji's anxious gaze. Beyond his shoulder her father had an equally anxious expression.

Shoji was rubbing her hand vigorously, not softly at all.

"Shoji? What happened?"

Shoji couldn't hide the relief that swept his features. Laying her hand down, he began to stroke her forehead softly, gently pushing the hair from her face.

"You fainted."

Frowning, Keiko tried to sit up, realizing as she did so that she was on one of the now set-up cots. Shoji supported her and she leaned her weight against him gratefully. Rubbing her forehead with one hand, she tiredly tried to get her mind to focus. She still felt groggy and reluctant to return to the real world when the dream one had been so beautiful.

Returning consciousness brought returning anguish. Her eyes inspected the cubicle they were now supposed to call home. Shivering, she turned back to the two men in her life. No use crying over spilled milk. What was done, was done, and nothing would change it now.

Her father's tired features brought her to her feet, where she had to pause as a wave of dizziness assailed her. Shoji wrapped a strong arm around her waist.

"Take it easy. We don't want to pick you up off the floor again."

Keiko studied the area mentioned and decided with distaste that she had no desire to be there again, either. Shrugging out of Shoji's hold, she rubbed her hands briskly together.

"So. Now what?" Wrinkling her nose with distaste, she studied the small apartment. "First things first. We need some way to clean this place."

Shoji felt a thrill of pride in his wife. She was stronger than she seemed, although he had wondered when he picked her up from the floor. His heart was just now slowing from its thundering pace that was a result of the terror he felt when he saw Keiko slump into unconsciousness.

Still, days of going without sleep and irregular meals that were rarely eaten had left a mark on all of them. Her body had finally succumbed to its need for respite.

Keiko went to her father, squeezing his shoulder reassuringly. "It's almost like camping out. Remember when Kenji and I put up a tent in the back yard?"

As she spoke, Keiko watched her father's face relax. "Hai. You were worried about the bugs, if I remember correctly."

Keiko grinned. "That wasn't the half of it. I was just as

concerned with four-legged critters as with six-legged ones."

When she turned to her husband, Keiko found him smiling. "Have you ever been camping?" she asked him.

Suddenly his eyes went blank. He turned away before answering. "Many years ago. When I was a boy and still living with my parents."

He began to unload a large bag that he had insisted Keiko keep with her at all times. Pulling out several shirts, he then produced several apples, a bag of peanuts, a box of tea, and several other food items.

Keiko's mouth dropped open in surprise. She hadn't even realized until now that she was hungry. When she knelt beside Shoji, he handed her a soft bundle, which, when she unwrapped it, happened to be a loaf of bread.

"What else do you have in there?" she asked curiously, trying to peer past him into the bag.

Instead of answering, he handed her another bundle. This time when she unrolled the shirt, several bills of different denominations fell into her lap.

Keiko's eyes went wide with surprise and she almost choked. "Where did you get this? Our bank account has been frozen for months now."

He shrugged, continuing to unload the sack.

"Shoji!" She was peeved at the way he continually refused to explain things to her.

When he turned his dark eyes her way, anger glittered just below the surface. Was he angry at her for asking? Well, that was just too bad. She had a right to know.

"My mother sent it to me."

"Oh."

Silence echoed around the room to suddenly be broken by the loud chattering of returning people.

"I'm afraid we missed supper," Shoji told her. His lips curled into a wry smile. "It seems we had other things on our minds."

An elderly woman peeked her head in their door, her little birdlike eyes taking in the occupants of the room. *"Konban wa."*

Both Shoji and her father rose to their feet. *"Hajimemashite,"* they answered her in unison, both bowing from their waists.

The little woman entered their apartment, her eyes roving over its barren desolation.

"I have cleaning supplies you can use," she told them. Keiko could have hugged her. "I get them for you now."

When she returned, she was carrying a bucket, mop, and broom. She handed them over to Keiko, who took them thankfully.

"Arigato," Keiko told her, and she saw the first hint of a smile on the old woman's face.

Nodding, she turned to Shoji. "They still a little wood and nails laying around if you think you can use. You must hurry before more people come."

Shoji's eyes went from the old woman to Keiko. Bowing, he turned to leave the room. Papa-san started to follow him. Both Keiko and Shoji tried to dissuade him, but he was resolute.

"I would only be in the way here," he told Keiko. "Perhaps I can be of some use to Shoji."

Since he was right, they didn't argue. The old woman watched them curiously, her bright eyes full of wisdom. Keiko had felt immediately drawn to her. She turned back to Keiko when the men had finally departed.

"You *nisei*. You speak Japanese?"

Keiko nodded. "Hai."

The old woman pursed her lips together. "Still, it better, I think, if we speak American. You agree?"

Keiko could understand her reasoning. These were perilous times, and they were part of an obviously paranoid country. Better to conform. Something in her rebelled at the thought.

"*Onamae wa?*" she asked, and the lady's eyes crinkled merrily back at her.

"My name Benko Kosugi. Everyone call me Obāsan."

The smile Keiko returned to her was full of warmth. She looked like a grandmother. "Well, Obāsan, I am Keiko Ibaragi."

Grinning, the old woman handed her the broom. "Make yourself useful, Keiko-san, and I see about getting a bucket of water."

She returned a short time later laden with an overflowing bucket. Keiko had already swept the compartment as clean as she possibly could, but it still looked dirty.

As Obāsan and Keiko worked, they got to know each other. The time flew, and by the time the men returned, Keiko knew that Obāsan was a widow now living with her son and his family. She also had a pretty accurate picture of Obāsan's background, from her homeland in Japan, to her son's occupation. She also found out that Obāsan's family lived just next door.

"My son, the American citizen," she told Keiko scornfully and then colored hotly when an angry voice rebuked her from the next cubicle.

"That's enough, Mama-san."

Keiko looked up to the top of the partition that extended down from the ceiling by at least twelve inches. She had expected to see a face there, but Obāsan's son obviously considered his verbal chastisement enough. It was soon apparent that there would be very little privacy afforded them in these tiny quarters.

After Obāsan left, Keiko helped Shoji and her father set up the other two cots. After that there was nothing left to do but wait for their other things to arrive.

Shoji handed Papa-san and Keiko each a slice of bread spread lavishly with jam. As they munched on their supper, Keiko couldn't help but wonder what would happen to them now. She had to be strong for her father's sake, if not for Shoji's. Sighing deeply, she turned to find her husband watching her.

"You are tired. Why don't you lay down for awhile?" He turned to her father. "You too, Papa-san."

Keiko frowned when her father did as he was bid without argument. His tired shoulders drooped dispiritedly. Keiko watched as his eyes slowly closed and his breathing became deep and even.

She turned her eyes back to her husband. "I couldn't sleep if I tried. I'm too keyed up."

Shoji shrugged his shoulders and walked to the corner, where he had dropped some wood.

"What are you going to do with that? And where did you ever get it?"

He bent to his task, answering her as he worked. "There were pieces left lying around from the construction they did here. The nails Papa-san and I found in the dirt. Hopefully there will be enough."

"For what?"

His look was enigmatic. "A table of some sort."

Since he had no hammer, he proceeded to pound together the boards with a large rock he had found. Keiko watched the way his muscles rippled with each blow of the rock. His strength, both physical and spiritual, was his greatest asset. She couldn't help but admire him.

A loud beeping outside sent Keiko scurrying to the door. A young Japanese boy climbed from the passenger side of an old army truck and began hauling out bundles. He smiled at Keiko. "Ibaragi?" he asked.

She could feel Shoji's presence behind her. "Hai," she answered him.

Nodding, he began lifting their luggage up the one step. Shoji reached around her to relieve the boy of his burden. When the last of the bundles had been unloaded, the boy tipped them a cheerful salute and climbed back in the truck, which roared off to its next rendezvous point.

Since she was dying for some tea, Keiko began by unloading the duffel bag. She lifted out the hot plate, thankful for Shoji's insistence on bringing it. Setting the plate aside, she looked around for some place to plug it in. There was nothing except the bulb hanging from the ceiling.

"I'll be finished in a minute," Shoji told her. "Then you can set the plate on the table and plug it into the light receptacle."

৵

Their first morning found them standing in line waiting to get into the mess hall, or cafeteria, as the government preferred to call it. There seemed to be little food, and what there was had so many additives to spread it around that it was hardly recognizable.

Thankfully, the government had sent them letters warning them to bring eating utensils and plates. Each person stood clutching their dishes and flatware, stoically biding their time until they could get inside to eat.

Over the next few months they would grow used to standing in long lines, but for now Keiko was growing impatient. She tapped her plate against her leg restlessly.

"Be still, Keiko-chan," her father admonished quietly, and again Keiko marveled at his serene countenance. Why was he so composed when she felt like she was walking on needles?

When they finally were inside, Keiko wondered just why she had been so anxious. The huge cavernous building reverberated with the din of hundreds of people talking and eating.

A spoonful of scrambled eggs was dumped on her plate, along with half a piece of bread and two Vienna sausages. There was no butter, no jam, nothing to make the dry bread more palatable.

After finishing her meal, such as it was, Keiko was still hungry. She had already found out that there were no seconds. Many of the people that were supposed to eat in this hall would go hungry or try another mess hall.

Keiko felt guilty for having eaten herself, although the flour that had been mixed in with the eggs to make them go further still clung to the roof of her mouth.

Shoji dumped his eggs on her plate. She glanced up at him in surprise.

"I'm not that hungry," he told her, but Keiko knew he was lying.

She pressed her lips together tightly. "Christians don't lie, Shoji." Pushing her plate toward him, she fixed him with a steely eye. "Now eat."

He was shaking his head, his chin set stubbornly. "No. You need it more."

Rising swiftly to her feet, Keiko placed her fists on her hips. "Then leave it," she told him implacably, "because I refuse to eat your food."

With that she turned and stalked toward the exit. He caught up with her before she could reach the door. Taking her by the arm, he pulled her to a stop.

"Come back to the table. I'll eat the sorry mess."

Her eyes went past him to her father, who was grinning with amusement. Reaching up, she touched Shoji's cheek with her fingertips.

"Go back and finish your meal. Someone else needs my seat. I'll just go back to the apartment and see about getting our dirty clothes together."

Shoji quickly surveyed the room. Every possible seat at the wooden picnic tables was occupied and still people were standing around waiting for a seat. Nodding his head sharply, he let her go.

Since Keiko had unpacked their bedding the night before, there was little for her to do. She gathered their laundry together and headed for the laundry room.

The lines here were as long as at the mess hall. Sighing, Keiko laid her bundle at her feet and waited for the next available tub.

Four hours later, she was still waiting. Impatience had turned to aggravation and then to a seething anger. The stoic features of the older *issei* women only exasperated her all the more. How could they accept their fate with so much aplomb?

Finally, Keiko reached the wash house only to find that they were expected to wash their clothes by hand. This didn't bother her as much as it obviously did some of the other *nisei* since she had always washed her clothes by hand, but it irritated her nonetheless, especially since all the hot water was long gone.

After scrubbing her clothes and rinsing them, she took them back to the apartment to dry them. Obãsan had already told her that she could use her clothing lines any time she chose.

She hung the clothes outside, watching the sky for any sign of rain. Dark clouds were once again forming across the horizon, causing Keiko to throw up a little word of prayer.

When she went inside, she found her father tending his bonsai tree. She glanced around. "Where's Shoji?"

"They gave him a job working at the mess hall," he informed her without looking up.

Surprised, Keiko crossed to the cot where he sat and seated herself beside him. She watched as he lovingly removed dead needles and trimmed some of the larger branches.

"Will he be gone all day?"

"Hai."

Keiko blew out her breath. Now what? What was she to do all day? Realizing she had missed lunch, she scrounged in the bag of food they had with them and found an apple.

"Do you want one, Papa-san?"

"Iie." Laying his scissors next to the small tree, he rose to his feet, rubbing his back with his hands. "I am meeting with a few of the men. I will be back later, but I am not sure when.

Do not worry about me, Keiko-chan. Understand?"

She dropped her eyes in the old way. "Hai," she agreed, but knew she wouldn't obey. How could she help but worry?

Taking the kettle, Keiko went to the wash room to fill it with water. When she returned, Benko was waiting for her.

"Would you like some tea, Obāsan?"

The little lady smiled warmly back at her. "That would be nice, Keiko-san."

Benko handed Keiko a small bundle. Keiko looked at her questioningly as she slowly unwrapped it.

"Some material I do not need. Perhaps you can make use of it."

Keiko's eyes filled with tears and she hugged the woman unabashedly. Benko would know that there was no privacy to be had at the bath houses nor at the latrines. Keiko had already suffered once from embarrassment as she realized that she would have to use the bathroom with no doors on the stalls. She had been pondering what to do when she noticed some of the women tacked either paper or swatches of material up when they used either. Since she had had neither, she had merely been thankful for the cover of darkness to hide her humiliation.

Shoji came home looking tired and grim. He told her that although there was a menu for each meal and that a truck delivered food for each meal, there was never enough and rarely what was on the menu.

"I watched the cook try to carve six hundred sixty pieces from one side of bacon."

Keiko could see that he was deep in thought. He left moments later, returning after about an hour without telling her where he had been.

❧

Their days became routine after that. Shoji would be paid twelve dollars a month for helping in the mess hall, but what good was money if you had no way to spend it?

Keiko later learned that things could be ordered from Sears & Roebuck or Montgomery Ward. Using some of their money, she ordered things to make their stall look more like a home. Although some people ordered linoleum and furniture, Shoji could see no sense in that when he knew their quarters were only temporary until the government had permanent locations built.

Still, Keiko ordered things that would give comfort to her father and help alleviate Shoji of some of his worry.

Thankfully, the weather was not too much of a concern. Although it seemed hot as the summer progressed, it was not unbearably so.

July came in with a lightning display that would rival any fireworks. Many of the families had arranged for their children to perform in a Fourth of July parade, so they were thankful that the day dawned warm and bright. How ironic that they could celebrate their freedom from the depths of a concentration camp.

The food situation had resolved itself after many weeks, especially when many people brought food to their friends in the camp.

Shoji's mother had shown up bringing food with her, as well. Keiko hadn't even known she had been and gone until she found the boxes in her apartment. She had been furious with Shoji for not telling her and allowing her to visit with the older Mrs. Ibaragi. Keiko genuinely liked Shoji's mother.

For his part, Shoji could not tell Keiko that his mother had arranged for freedom for Keiko and himself, but had not been able to manage it for Tochigi-san. He knew Keiko would never agree, and since coming here he had watched Keiko's bitterness toward the American government grow.

Sure she had the right, but it was doing no one any good, least of all Keiko.

Toward the end of August, word came that they would soon be

moved. No one knew where, and no one knew exactly when.

For three days it rained, and by the time it stopped, Keiko had a cold that left her feeling miserable. She stayed in her cot most of the day. When Shoji came home, he fixed her some canned soup.

Squatting on his haunches beside her cot, he gently brushed the damp hair away from her face. "At least your fever is gone," he told her softly. She tried to smile, but he could see it was just too much effort.

Shoji kissed her lightly on her lips, hoping that when her sickness left, so would her lethargy. She had been so unlike herself the past few weeks he was really beginning to worry.

Sitting on the floor beside her, he pulled his Bible from the table and began to read out loud. After reading a few verses, he turned to find her gently snoring. Smiling, he laid the Bible aside.

When Keiko awoke, the apartment was empty. Her father was once more with the other men, trying to beautify the grounds. That they were somewhat successful was a testament to their grit and determination.

She supposed Shoji was helping. He often did when he wasn't at the mess hall. Getting up, Keiko went to the door, throwing it wide. Sitting on the step, she watched the hustle and bustle around her.

Women were washing their clothes and tending their children. Men were busy working at whatever their hands could find to do. It was no wonder the place had begun to look less like a racetrack and more like a community.

With something of a shock, Keiko realized that she had done nothing toward making this so. For weeks now she had been busy feeling sorry for herself.

Even Papa-san had made the best of the situation, and he was the one she thought would be least likely to survive the ordeal. His strength came from within and was not dependent on circumstances.

Overcome with guilt, Keiko threw her head back, staring at the vibrant blue sky. "I haven't done very well, have I Lord?" she asked, her voice rising up into the heavens. "Forgive me, Lord," she whispered. "I'll try to do better. Help me to think less of me."

Keiko soon realized that the men worked not because it was necessary, but because they wanted to. They wanted to make this place the best that they could for their family and loved ones.

❧

Word came that they would soon be uprooted. They had only a few days to prepare, but what was there to prepare?

Many had more to take out than what they had brought in, including Keiko, but somehow things seemed different. There was no longer the fear of what they would have to withstand, but instead a fear of the future.

When it came time to leave, they were loaded on a train just a block from the racetrack. The windows were nailed shut, as were the shutters.

Keiko huddled against her husband, the dusky interior of the train leaving her feeling gloomy and morose. A guard moved purposefully up and down the cars. It was obvious to everyone that they were not a threat, or there would have been more military.

The *issei* attitude of *shikata ga nai*, nothing can be done, had nearly driven Keiko crazy at first. Now she realized that it was that very perspective that helped them to survive.

As the train rattled its way along the track, Keiko felt that her teeth would surely be rattled from her head any minute. The old train had obviously seen better days.

Hour after hour passed with little relief from the horrible monotony. Children whined fretfully at their forced inactivity. Keiko leaned back and gave her mind over to its thoughts. Would Obāsan be coming later to wherever it was they were being sent? She had not been sent on this train, so Keiko had no idea.

Shoji curled an arm around her shoulder, pulling her head down to his shoulder. "Why don't you try to get some sleep?"

Keiko hid a grin. He had to be kidding. But when she looked at her father, she found his head drooping to the side and he was sound asleep.

Deciding to humor her husband, she closed her eyes, but sleep would not come. Instead she let her thoughts roam freely. What would they find at the end of this trip? More importantly, where were they going?

The farther they traveled, the more the heat intensified until the train seemed like a traveling sweatbox. There was a distinguishable difference in the sound of the train moving across the tracks, but Keiko's untutored mind could not tell what it was.

"We're crossing the Colorado," the guard told them, and for the first time they had an inkling of which direction they were headed. East.

Several hours later the train began to slow, then pulled to a stop. As they disembarked, Keiko's eyes hurt from trying to adjust to the intensity of the sun after the dark interior of the train. And the heat. Roiling waves of it seemed to billow all around them. Sweat poured from their bodies, making Keiko long for a cool drink.

"Where are we?" she asked Shoji, and he motioned to an old water tower in the distance. Across its silver surface, Keiko could read the faded, black letters. CASA GRANDE, ARIZONA.

ten

Shoji picked the last of the cotton in the row then stood stiffly to his feet. Although he was in good physical condition, picking cotton was backbreaking work. How must the older men be feeling if he was stiff and sore?

He stood for a moment, watching the others. For the most part they moved swiftly and efficiently. Only a few straggled behind. Even the older men worked diligently not far in back of him. It was rare for Shoji not to receive the extra three dollars incentive money for the most cotton picked in a day, not because he particularly needed it, but because his energy drove him relentlessly on.

Shoji wondered how Keiko was managing. His lips curled up at the edges and his eyes took on a decided glow.

She had certainly surprised him. Somehow she had mysteriously transformed from a shy, quiet girl to a forceful, determined young woman. The change both mystified and delighted him.

When they had arrived, Keiko had immediately jumped in to help turn this barren desert into a remarkable community. Although many buildings had not been completed when they arrived, and still weren't for that matter, Keiko and Papa-san had tried to rally their block in the relocation center into a living, thriving community.

Already many noticeable changes had been accomplished in the short time they had been here. Two long months. He glared at the sky. How long, Lord? How much longer?

In the beginning he had worked in the mess hall, but when the surrounding farmers had asked for volunteers to pick cotton, he had jumped at the chance. When he was picking cotton, he was on the outside. It was amazing how confining even such a large area as Gila River, or Butte Camp as others called it, could feel.

Imagine. A concentration camp, and it was still the third largest city in Arizona. Shoji grinned wryly. He would be willing to wager a lot that the good people of Arizona weren't exactly thrilled with the news.

A throbbing drone in the distance brought his eyes swiveling around. His lips set grimly. Often they could see the B17 bombers practicing in the distance, dropping their bombs of flour on the surrounding fields.

Shoji knew it shouldn't bother him, but it did. Someday those planes would fly over Japan and kill many people, some of them possibly friends that he went to school with.

He knew Keiko would be appalled at his thoughts. She would consider them un-American. Perhaps they were. He didn't wish America to lose the war, he only wished his friends and his father's family not to, either. That part of him that was Japanese cried for the country of his father's birth. A beautiful land with a mostly gentle race of people.

But he knew also the stubborn dedication of that people. They would not give up their quest easily.

How had this war come about, anyway? He still wasn't sure. All he knew was that the Japanese were suffering both here and abroad.

When he handed in his pickings, he wasn't surprised to find that he again had earned an extra three dollars. Smiling slightly, he pocketed the money in his jeans, thinking of what Keiko would do with the money.

Since they still had the money he had brought with them when they went to Tulare, they didn't really need much. The government provided food, and that had certainly improved over what they had received at Tulare. Many things were different and better here than they had been there.

Keiko had asked him if they might share the money he

earned with others in their block who had larger families and less income. He had been surprised, but he had readily agreed. The warm smile she had given him had made him warm all over. Even now, thinking about it brought a new rush of feeling.

He had been right. Keiko had been easy to love. There was no denying it. He was hopelessly, irrevocably, crazily in love with his wife. He looked forward to returning to her each evening, and although they had army bunks and didn't sleep together, he still felt her presence keenly.

As usual, it was late when he returned. Supper was long past, but Shoji knew Keiko would have something prepared for him. His mother was continually sending them packages of food and items she thought they could use. That, added to the fact that Gila was an agricultural center, made it relatively easy to procure food.

Some of the Japanese even traded with the Pima Indians. He could still remember Keiko's face when a friend had shared his tamales with them. Shoji grinned to himself. He thought for sure Keiko's eyes would pop from her head. Since Shoji was used to the spices of Japan, the tamales had seemed mild to him, but Keiko was not used to such heat. Ever since, whenever her friend shared his tamales, Keiko saved them for Papa-san and himself.

He climbed the porch step to their door and went inside. A happy feeling washed over him at the warm interior. Already fall was sending its freezing temperatures to the desert at night. The contrast between days and nights was remarkable.

Keiko came from behind the blanket they had put up as a curtain to separate their living quarters from their sleeping quarters. She stopped, surprised to see him.

"I didn't hear you come in."

He dropped his lunch sack on the table he had built from the excess lumber lying around the facility. Although others had taken lumber from the stacks piled up for buildings, he had limited himself to the scraps he found.

It had taken time, but eventually he had managed to build a table, three chairs, a cupboard each for Papa-san and he and Keiko's clothes, shelves for the walls, and a storage cabinet. His furniture was not nearly as elaborate as some had made, but it was well built and sturdy.

Keiko went to the little oil stove the army had provided and lifted a pot from its surface. She dished the stew onto a plate and Shoji's mouth watered appreciatively.

"Smells good."

Keiko grinned. "I'm afraid it's just fish stew. Little Ishimi caught some catfish in the canal." She lowered her voice to a whisper. "Don't tell anyone."

Shoji frowned. "He could get in big trouble if he's caught."

Shrugging, Keiko laid the bowl in front of him. "They're not as strict with the security around here as they used to be. I think most people realize that the Japanese are no threat to them."

After washing his hands in the wash bowl Keiko provided, Shoji sat down at the table and began to hungrily devour the food. It had been a long time since lunch.

"Where's Papa-san?"

Keiko handed him a bowl of rice and some bread. "He went to a block manager's meeting. He may be late."

Shoji stopped chewing, his brows coming together. "Not later than ten?"

Keiko placed her fists on her hips. "You know Papa-san wouldn't miss curfew. What's bothering you?"

Shoji resumed eating. How could he answer such a question? How could he tell her that every time he saw the B17s practicing their bombing runs he felt unsettled?

"It's nothing," he finally told her. "I just worry, that's all."

Keiko slid into the chair opposite him, eager to share her day. This was Shoji's favorite time of the evening. He loved listening to her tales of the people and the situations they could get themselves into.

"So what else did little Ishimi get himself into today?"

Wrinkling her nose, Keiko proceeded to tell him how the little boy had thought perhaps Keiko would like to have a lizard for a pet. Shoji grinned.

"And how did you get yourself out of that one?"

"I told him the poor thing would probably miss his mama so much he would just up and die."

Shoji's grin turned to laughter. "Leave it to you."

Keiko watched her husband and felt a spiral of warmth work its way throughout her body. She loved Shoji's laugh. When he laughed, he forgot to be inscrutable, and his mahogany eyes grew bright with his feelings.

She was so intent on her thoughts she didn't realize that Shoji had asked her a question. Color flooded her cheeks.

"What did you say?"

One eyebrow winged its way upward and a small smile tilted the corner of his lips. "It's not important."

Coming around the table, Shoji lifted Keiko to her feet and into his arms. He grinned down at her surprised face before settling his lips across hers in a soft kiss.

Keiko was so surprised that for a moment she hung limp in his arms. Surprise gave way to desire and Keiko found herself kissing Shoji back in a way they hadn't shared for a long time.

When Shoji felt Keiko's response, his lips became more demanding. Sliding his hands across Keiko's back, he found himself wanting to pull her closer and even closer still. He couldn't seem to get enough of her.

Just when reason was about to leave him, Shoji heard a sound at their door. Pulling back, he set Keiko away from him and returned to his seat at the table.

Keiko sank gratefully into her own chair, her legs like noodles beneath her. The pupils of her eyes were still dilated with desire and it took her a moment to compose herself.

Papa-san came in the door, his eyes going from one to the other.

"How did you do in the fields today, Shoji-san?"

Shoji looked up in surprise as if he had almost forgotten. Pulling the money from his pockets, he threw it on the table.

Keiko looked at the six dollars and shook her head. "You had the most again today?"

"Hai." Shoji nodded to the money. "It's yours. Do with it what you wish."

Her warm eyes sought his. "Is there nothing you need?"

His intense look brought color flooding to her cheeks. "Nothing that money can buy."

Papa-san coughed softly. "If you will excuse me, I think I will go to bed now."

"It's only six o'clock, Papa-san," Keiko admonished him. "You can't possibly be tired."

"I am, actually," he told her, and for the first time Keiko noticed the tired lines fanning out from his eyes. There were times when she forgot that he was still recovering from a heart attack.

Noticing her distress, Tochigi-san waved a hand airily in her direction. "Now do not start worrying about me. I think I may be catching a cold, that's all."

Keiko said nothing, but she determined to watch her father carefully for the next few days. How she would get him to behave himself was beyond her, but she would manage it somehow.

When they were all in bed that night, Keiko was painfully aware of the distance that separated her from her husband. Only a few feet, but it may as well have been miles. What would have happened if her father had not arrived when he did?

Shoji had told her he didn't want to take the chance of conceiving a child in a concentration camp. Had he perhaps changed his mind? Her heart raced faster at the prospect. One was never sure where Shoji was concerned.

The next day the linoleum arrived. Keiko was thrilled. Already many of her neighbors had procured the flooring, but she had waited, choosing to spend her money on other things.

Since the camp had been built with mostly green pine, as it dried, huge cracks formed between the slats, leaving gaping holes that just begged the dust to come in. It wouldn't have been so bad if it hadn't been for the dust storms.

Dust blew in from every direction, getting in everything and everywhere. The linoleum helped some, but when the wind blew, nothing stopped the sand in its relentless march.

Keiko moved the furniture and unrolled the flooring. It gave her immense satisfaction when she was finished. Slapping her hands together, she smiled widely.

"There. Now let's see the dust come up through the cracks."

One thing she was heartily thankful for was the fact that the weather had finally cooled off and the thunderstorms from the summer monsoon had subsided. If the heat didn't kill you, the humidity would. Now temperatures continued to drop and the air was long past dry.

At night the temperatures dropped so low that water would freeze in the buckets. Fortunately, they had an oil stove to keep them warm.

A letter arrived from Sumiko, and Keiko eagerly tore it open.

November 11, 1942

Dear Kay,

How's the weather out there? Is there anything worse than a desert? Boy, how I miss the green fields of California.

The food here is awful, the living conditions primitive, and the facilities inadequate. Other than that, things are great.

Did you hear about John Parker? He was drafted

and sent to Europe somewhere. France, I think. His dad tried everything he could to get him out of it, but I guess he didn't have enough clout.

Now for the good news. You're going to be an aunt. Isn't that wonderful? Ken is so excited.

Imagine. Me, a mother. I can hardly wait. I know you'll tell Papa-san for us. Let me know what he says.

I guess I better go for now. I have to get ready for school. I'm helping to teach second grade. The kids are great, but mischievous. They don't like Mrs. Carson, who is the main teacher. I don't know why. She's a nice enough lady. I think maybe it's because she's white.

Give that hunk of Japanese manhood a big kiss for me, and Papa-san, too.

> *Love ya,*
> *Sue*

When Keiko finished the letter, there were tears in her eyes. Oh how she missed Sumiko and Kenji. Papa-san would be thrilled, she knew, but what would Shoji have to say? If Kenji was excited about the baby, would that perhaps make Shoji reconsider his position? If there was one thing Keiko wanted more than anything, it was Shoji's baby.

She wasn't sure how it had come about, or when, but she knew now without a doubt that she loved her husband.

She found out later that evening what his reaction would be. If anything, Shoji's eyes became once again enigmatic, and he seemed to draw even further away from her.

Papa-san, on the other hand, was ecstatic. He couldn't wait to share the news with his friends that he was about to become an *ojiisan*. His pride knew no bounds, but the looks he threw at Keiko and Shoji were speculative, to say the least.

The weather grew progressively cooler until temperatures

were cold both day and night. Keiko used the four-dollar allowance she received for each of them to order winter clothes from the Sears catalog.

A box arrived from Shoji's mother, only Mrs. Ibaragi brought it herself. Shoji stared in surprise at his mother waiting in the administration office.

"What are you doing here?"

She looked around, before arching an eyebrow. "Is there somewhere we can go to talk?"

Picking up the box, Shoji led the way along the barracks until they reached barracks forty. The door to apartment C was closed firmly against the cold temperatures. Leading his mother inside, Shoji watched as she studied her surroundings. When she turned to him, there were tears in her eyes.

"How can you stand it?"

His lips pressed tightly together. Setting the box on the floor, he straightened and went to the stove to light it.

"What are you doing here, Mother?"

Without being asked, Mrs. Ibaragi pulled out one of the seats from the table. Lowering herself against the sunny yellow seat cushion that Keiko had made, she settled her purse on the table.

"I want to get you out of here. You and Keiko." Seeing the look in her son's eyes, she rushed on. "I know Keiko doesn't want to leave her father, and I still haven't managed to arrange for his leave. But if we can make Keiko understand her chances of getting her father out will be better if she is on the outside. . ."

The anger in Shoji's eyes communicated itself to his mother. "None of this makes any sense," he told her. "Did you know that here in Arizona many Japanese were never sent to camps? They're still free. While others. . .others lose everything. It just doesn't make sense."

"I know. In Hawaii, where there are more Japanese than anywhere else, and where they would have the most cause for such actions, most of the Japanese haven't been relocated."

Shoji brushed a hand in agitation through his hair. "It has to be because of the land in California." He gritted his teeth. "Did you do as I asked about the farm?"

She got to her feet. "Yes, I purchased the farm for you. Does Keiko know?"

He turned on her. "No, and I don't want her to. If Keiko learns to love me, I want it to be without obligations."

Mrs. Ibaragi placed a hand on her son's arm. "And what about leaving here? Your grandfather pulled a lot of strings to get you and Keiko set free."

Shoji looked less than pleased. "Tell him thanks, but no thanks. Keiko and I will stay here."

"Shoji. . ." she implored, using the name he preferred.

"Forget it, Mother," he snapped. "If Papa-san cannot go, then neither do we."

Sighing, she pressed her lips tightly together. "You're as stubborn as your father."

He opened his mouth to answer her, when the door opened and Keiko came in. Her eyes lit up when she saw Mrs. Ibaragi.

"Mrs. Ibaragi! What are you doing here?"

Receiving a speaking look from her son, Mrs. Ibaragi went and took Keiko in her arms.

"I came to see if everything is all right with you two."

Keiko smiled softly. "We are well, as you can see." Keiko's eyes went to her husband. "You are not in the fields today?"

He shook his head. "No. There is no more cotton to be picked. I will be starting to work at the model factory tomorrow."

"Model factory?" Shoji's mother retreated to her previous chair, while Keiko set about fixing them some tea.

Keiko nodded. "Hai. They make models of ships and planes that the military use in their operations."

Mrs. Ibaragi turned to her son. "You should like that.

You've always liked working with wood."

"Maybe."

Shoji's noncommittal answer hid the real reason for his reluctance. True, he knew he would enjoy the work, but those models represented ships and planes that might very well hold a friend. Of course, the same could be said of the American models. Sighing, he turned away. Whichever way this war went, someone he loved would suffer.

Shoji's mother left, but not before arguing again with her son. He walked her back to the administration building where her rented car was parked. Kissing her, he closed the door firmly behind her, not sure that he was doing the right thing for Keiko.

&

Shoji's mother showed up again for Thanksgiving. Having received a permit to do so, she took Keiko, Shoji, and Papa-san to Phoenix to have dinner in one of the hotels.

For Keiko the experience was bittersweet. It had been so long since she had had turkey, she almost forgot what it tasted like. The bitter came in knowing that no matter what the atmosphere in the restaurant, they had to return to Camp Butte.

They could just as easily walk out the door and never return, but what would that accomplish? Only when this crazy war ended would life make any sense again. Maybe not then. Who knew what would happen to them after the war?

Mrs. Ibaragi told them that she wouldn't be able to come for Christmas, but she sent them all Christmas presents anyway.

&

Keiko was wearing her new dress when Shoji came in from outside. His eyes swept over her in a brief appraisal before his lashes swept down to hide his eyes.

Keiko knew that the pink chiffon was becoming. She was irritated that Shoji said nothing.

"We got a card from Kenji and Sumiko," she told him.

"How are they doing?"

Keiko began to set the table with the new dishes Mrs. Ibaragi had sent.

"Sumiko said that it's really cold there in Utah. She said the government provided stoves, but they didn't install them. They are sitting outside beside the door, but no one is supposed to install them. They're supposed to wait for the government engineers to do it."

Shoji snorted. "That could very well be after the war ends. What are they doing for heat?"

"Sumiko said that Kenji installed it anyway. It seems they have a harder time getting food than we do, too."

Shoji took the plates from her hands and set them on the table. He took her hands into his own, kissing each one softly. Keiko felt her heart drop to her feet.

"Don't worry Keiko-chan. They'll be okay," he told her softly. "There's nothing you can do. They can order things, just like we can. They get money just like we do. They'll be okay."

Sucking in her breath, she nodded her head. "I suppose you're right. But I think I'll do some heavy praying nonetheless."

"I'll join you," he told her, and did.

January 1943 rolled around and Keiko tried to celebrate it for her father's sake. They had no bills to pay, and the apartment was only twenty feet by twenty feet, but Keiko cleaned it thoroughly anyway.

She managed to find the fixings for the *ozoni* and *mochi*, but the buckwheat pancakes were beyond her. At least Butte Camp had plenty of agriculture to allow them vegetables. Even *daikon* was grown here to be shipped to all nine of the other relocation camps.

When spring came, it came softly to the desert. Keiko was amazed that a barren land could suddenly be so filled with color. Even the birds returned to the region full of vibrancy and vitality. Keiko envied them their freedom.

April brought with it shower upon shower. Keiko hadn't seen so much rain since last summer's monsoon. She didn't mind because it helped the lawns the families had planted between the barracks. Since Gila River was used for farming, there was plenty of water to supply the camp's needs; however, the rain was an added blessing. Except for all the mud that was a result.

Keiko wandered to the mess hall for lunch. Shoji was again in the fields, and Keiko felt the desire for some company. Her father was constantly busy with friends his own age. They were issei. They understood each other.

Shaking her head, Keiko grinned wryly. She was glad somebody understood them.

After receiving her food, she looked for an empty place to sit. Amazingly, she found an empty table, but she knew it wouldn't be empty for long.

There was a commotion over by the doors, but Keiko ignored it. She was busy trying to find one of her friends to talk to. Suddenly, someone was standing next to her elbow.

"May I sit here?"

Keiko looked up at the white-haired woman standing next to her and the many men surrounding her. Her shrewd eyes studied Keiko thoughtfully.

Rising quickly to her feet, Keiko almost spilled her plate.

"Mrs. Roosevelt."

The woman smiled slightly. "That I am. May I sit with you?"

Flustered, Keiko looked from her to her companions and back again. "Of course. Please. Have a seat."

Mrs. Roosevelt sat down across from Keiko, ignoring her traveling companions. Her bright eyes appraised Keiko slowly.

"Have you been here long?" she wanted to know.

"Long enough," Keiko answered her stiffly.

The woman wasn't the least embarrassed. Nodding her head, she began to eat.

"These are sad times for our country."

Keiko snorted. "For some more than others."

Mrs. Roosevelt's birdlike eyes twinkled back at her. "You surely have reason to be bitter. I know that I would."

"Would you?"

The old woman's eyes flashed at the question. "There are many things in this life that aren't fair. Life is not fair. But life is what you make it. It can defeat you, or you can defeat it."

Realizing that she had offended the president's wife, Keiko dropped her eyes. When she looked back up, she had her feelings under control.

"Mrs. Roosevelt, God is in control of this world. Mr. Hirohito may think he is. Mr. Hitler may think that he is. Mr. Roosevelt may think that he is. But they aren't. You're right, Mrs. Roosevelt. Life is not fair. Only God is."

Rising swiftly to her feet, Keiko left the woman sitting with her mouth slightly open.

eleven

For the next several days, Keiko continually berated herself for losing her temper with the president's wife. What had she accomplished by her actions? Nothing! If only she had held her bitterness and temper in check, she might have been able to better help those from Gila River who needed it.

Dropping her knitting on the table, she got to her feet and began to pace. Everything was so unsettled, not the least of which was her relationship with her husband. At times she felt as though she were on a whirling merry-go-round.

Going back to the table, she reached for the baby blanket she was knitting for Sumiko. Her fingers trailed gently across the soft material, her eyes taking on a faraway look.

How long could this war go on? She hoped not much longer because she longed with every fiber of her being to begin a family. But as for now, Shoji wouldn't hear of it.

She had to get out of here for awhile. The very walls seemed to be closing in on her. Leaving a note for her father, she hastened outside and headed in the direction of barracks fifty-nine.

Benko Kosugi had arrived shortly after Keiko, and although she lived a considerable distance away, Keiko and the old woman spent much time together.

When Keiko knocked on the door of apartment 6B, the door was flung open by a young girl. Keiko recognized Obāsan's granddaughter and smiled.

"Hello, Mayumi. Is Obāsan here?"

The girl's eyes brightened. "Hi, Keiko. Sure, come on in." Turning, Mayumi yelled over her shoulder. "Obāsan! Keiko's here."

Benko came from the rear, tut-tutting at her granddaughter. "Such manners, Mayumi."

The girl's eyes met Keiko's. Rolling them, she shrugged her shoulders, passing Keiko on her way out.

When Keiko was sitting across from Benko with a cup of tea in front of her, she didn't really know what to say. What had brought her here in such a hurry anyway?

"So, Keiko-san. How is Shoji-san?"

"Fine, Obāsan," she answered the old woman absently.

"And your father?"

Perhaps that was the crux of the matter. For days now her father had been listless. Pale. Keiko's eyes probed Obāsan's.

"Your son is a doctor."

Benko nodded, her wise eyes flittering across Keiko's face. "You wish him to look at Tochigi-san?"

Keiko blew air from her lips, causing the bangs on her forehead to stir. "I don't think Papa-san would allow it."

Obāsan leaned back, understanding filling her expression.

"Ah. You wish him do it without your father's knowledge."

Tracing a pattern on the tablecloth with her fingers, Keiko couldn't meet Obāsan's eyes. She knew that being issei herself she would think it untoward that the daughter should try to rule the father.

Benko reached a hand across the table, folding Keiko's fingers into her own. "I will ask him, Keiko-san. We see what we can do."

Relieved, Keiko got to her feet. "*Arigato*, Obāsan. *Arigato*."

Keiko left the old woman standing on her little porch. She had as much love for Benko as if she were her real grandmother.

Stopping by the post office, Keiko found another letter from Sumiko. Her eyes sparkled as she hurried home to read it. Only this time, the mood of the letter was much more somber.

May 7, 1943

Dear Kay,

I am pleased that Papa-san was so happy with our news. Now I have some bad news to share with you.

Ken has decided to join the army and go overseas. I was angry at first. Why should he fight for a country that would deny its people their due process of law and force them to be interned in such awful conditions?

But Ken explained to me that even when your government does something stupid, you don't stop loving your country. If that were the case, no one would ever serve their country, because the government is always making stupid mistakes.

I didn't want him to go, especially now with the baby coming, but I understand his need to give something back to the country that has given us so much.

Look out, Hirohito! My Kenji is coming.

Look out, Mr. Hitler, the Americans are coming to pay you a visit.

Take care of yourself. We love you.
Sue and Ken

P.S. Do you have any news for me yet? Hmmm?

Keiko crushed the letter in her hand, her face as white as the proverbial sheet. *Not Kenji! Dear God, not Kenji!*

When Shoji arrived home that night, he found his wife distraught and distant. There were traces of tears on her cheeks. Frowning, he tried to take her in his arms, but she pulled away from him.

"Keiko, what's wrong?"

She threw a piece of paper at him. "Here. Read this."

He watched her piddle about the apartment, straightening things that didn't need to be straightened, cleaning a table that was already clean.

Sumiko's letters were always short, but they always packed a wallop. Grimacing, he dropped the crumpled sheet on the storage cabinet. He didn't say anything. What was there to say? He admired Kenji his noble sentiments, was proud of his courage, but there was nothing he could do, nothing he would want to do. Except perhaps comfort Keiko.

Why had she pushed him away? What thoughts were going through her head now? Every time he thought he was making headway with her, something happened to set them back in their relationship.

❧

When they went to the mess hall that evening, the atmosphere in the building was tense. Keiko noticed many glances thrown their way. Papa-san seemed to see nothing amiss, enjoying his meal with a relish he hadn't shown in a long time.

A young man came to their table, bowing slightly from the waist. "Tochigi-san. We have received word from Mr. Dillon Myer, the director of the War Relocation Authority, that some evacuees are to be sent to Tule Lake in California. Is this true?"

At the mention of what was considered the Japanese correctional facility, Papa-san's face became more inscrutable than Keiko had ever seen Shoji's. His eyes darkened in anger.

"Am I not to be allowed to eat my meal in peace? Must you take this opportunity to question me on such matters?"

The young man flushed scarlet. "I am sorry, but you are the block manager."

Tochigi-san fixed him with a steely eye. "Then be at the block meeting tonight. We will discuss it then."

Looking from Keiko to Shoji and back to Papa-san, he nodded his head and turned to go. When Papa-san glanced up, he caught Shoji's eye. A message flashed between them, and

Keiko felt a little thrill of fear.

"What's going on?" she demanded.

Her father continued to eat his meal. "Eat your food, Keiko, before it gets cold."

She turned to her husband. "Shoji?"

He looked down at his own plate. "Nothing you need to worry about."

Angry, Keiko rose slowly to her feet. She dumped the contents of her plate onto Shoji's. "When will you ever start to treat me as something other than a child?" She glared at his down-bent head. "Fine. Enjoy your meal. But I will be at that block meeting tonight, also."

Shoji watched her walk away with a great deal of irritation. Why couldn't Keiko trust him to do what was best for both of them? For all of them?

His eyes came back to Papa-san's and he saw the sympathy there. "She never has liked to be managed."

"I wonder where she gets it from?"

Papa-san cackled gleefully, and Shoji grinned as he rose to his feet.

"I have no doubt that you can control her," Papa-san told him.

The smile left Shoji's face. "I don't want to control her. I want a partner in my marriage, not a slave."

The gray eyebrows lifted upward, and Shoji felt himself color hotly. If what he said was true, then why hadn't he talked with Keiko when she had wanted him to? Seeking to right the wrong he had just committed, Shoji bowed and quickly left his father-in-law.

He found Keiko getting ready to go out the door of their apartment.

"I want to talk to you," he told her softly.

She fixed him with a scathing look. "I don't have time. I promised Benko I would stop by and see her, so I need to go now to be back in time for the block meeting."

"You're not going to any block meeting," he told her, but for once his words had no effect whatsoever on Keiko. She tried to push past him, but he gripped her arm in a hold that was gentle, but nonetheless unyielding.

"I want to talk to you," he repeated.

She looked from his hand holding her arm back to his face. Her look was eloquent.

Letting go of her arm, Shoji pulled out a chair at the table for her. She settled herself against it, her eyes going to Shoji's face.

"You already know that the government came to our camp in February and March to offer us enlistment in the army."

She nodded.

"Well, many of the young men refused to sign up. There was a form that needed to be filled out. Question 27 asked if we would be willing to serve in the army, and question 28 asked if we would renounce all loyalty to Japan and swear allegiance to the United States of America."

He glanced at her to see if she was following him so far. Her intelligent brown eyes stared back at him.

"And what did you say?"

Here it came, he just knew it. The explosion to end all explosions. "I answered no to the first, and yes to the second."

Keiko swallowed hard. "And just exactly what does that mean?"

"We have been separated into groups. The yes-yes, no-no, and yes-no."

"You mean some actually refused to swear allegiance to America?"

"Hai. Mainly the *kibei* and *issei*. But others who are loyal to America still refuse to serve in her armed services. They want no part of a country that would treat them like criminals just because of their race."

"Like Sumiko."

Nodding, Shoji took her hand, hoping he could make her

understand. "Keiko, I refused to serve in the armed services not because of loyalty, but because I cannot bear the thought that I might be responsible for the death of a friend or loved one. I have many friends and family in Japan. Can you understand?"

She studied him for a long time, and he felt his mouth go dry. Sliding her hand from beneath his, she rose to her feet looking down at him.

"I understand," she told him softly. "It must be hard for you. But let me ask you something, Shoji. What happens if the Japanese win this war? What then?"

She went quickly from the room and didn't look back. For the first time, Shoji actually considered what the United States losing this war would mean. The thought was a chilling one.

≈

Keiko walked across the roads that connected the barracks, oblivious to where she was going. The air around her grew warmer and perspiration began to run in rivulets down her back.

When the wind started to blow slightly, she was thankful for the breeze. Lifting her long dark hair from her shoulders, she balled it into a bun on top of her head, twisting it so that it would stay.

She should be thankful that Shoji wasn't going to be sent to Europe. Thankful that he wouldn't be killed on a foreign battlefield, fighting an enemy he considered no enemy at all.

Her path took her away from the barracks and toward the front gate. Guard towers stood sentry, but the soldier on duty was not concerned with her. His eyes were focused across the barren desert toward the mountains in the distance.

Following his gaze, Keiko could see a brown column of dust rising into the air for as far as the eye could see. Her heart dropped. A dust storm. They came suddenly, attacked fiercely, and receded just as quickly. From its rapid advancement she could tell she probably wouldn't have time to make it back to their apartment.

Glancing quickly around, she tried to decide her best course of action. Already the wind was picking up and the air was starting to cool.

If the storm was followed by rain, flash floods would more than likely occur in the vicinity. She stared harder, but she couldn't tell if this storm had rain behind it.

Before she could decide, Keiko saw little Ishimi struggling against the wind, which was growing stronger by the minute. She hurried to his side, kneeling beside him.

"Ishimi, what are you doing so far from home?"

Relief flashed momentarily in his eyes. He held one arm up and Keiko could see the string of catfish the boy had caught in the canal.

"We have to get you home." Already Keiko had to yell to be heard above the wind. They were still a long way from the nearest barracks and the first traces of sand were stinging against their skin.

"Hurry, Ishimi."

Taking the boy by the hand, Keiko tried to hasten them in the general direction of where she knew the barracks to be. If only they could get to the barracks, someone would give them shelter.

In moments vision was impossible. Sand swirled angrily about them, refusing to allow them to turn in any direction. Keiko couldn't tell which direction was which. She clung to Ishimi, afraid that she would lose him.

The wind was so strong, pieces of debris scuttled across the compound around them. Fearing for their safety, Keiko pulled the little boy closer, trying to protect him as much as possible.

Ishimi clung to her legs. "I can't see!" He hollered, rubbing his eyes with the backs of his fist.

"I know," Keiko yelled back. "Hang on to me tight, Ishimi.

Don't let go, whatever you do."

Fighting her way against the wind, Keiko pushed forward, hoping she was going in the right direction. She would hate to find herself out in the middle of the desert when this was all over.

What seemed like hours later, she bumped into a structure, hugging it in her relief. Shuffling her hands along its surface, Keiko soon found herself in front of the administration building. She struggled with the door, but it was already locked.

Of course. It was after five o'clock. The warehouse buildings next door would be closed, too. Trying not to panic, Keiko stopped, willing herself to remain calm.

For a moment the storm seemed to abate, and in that moment Keiko thought she heard her name being called. Lifting her head, she listened harder. She could faintly hear a voice being blown away from her in the distance.

"Here! We're over here!" she screamed back. Could they hear her? What was more, could anyone ever hope to find them in this chaos?

What seemed like an eternity later, a body appeared at her side. Strong arms wrapped securely around her and Keiko sagged with relief.

"Shoji! Thank God you found us."

"Us?"

Keiko pulled Ishimi into the safety of their embrace. Without warning the sand stopped blowing only to be followed a moment later by a torrent of water, drenching them within seconds.

"There's no time to get to a barracks. Get down."

Shoving both Keiko and Ishimi toward the ground, Shoji tried to get them as far under the building as possible. Flashes of lightning lit up the sky, followed by resounding booms of thunder.

Since the buildings were built somewhat on supports, there

was a small space to crawl beneath. Ishimi fit his body almost entirely under the building, whereas Keiko and Shoji could only get halfway.

Shoji tried to shield their bodies as much as possible from the elements. Previous encounters with dust storms convinced him that hail wasn't far behind.

Half-inch balls of ice began to pelt the ground around them. Shoji grimaced as they hit his back like little shots of fire. Keiko gasped when a pellet found tender skin.

Before long the hail stopped, but the rain continued. Water was rapidly filling the areas beneath the buildings.

"Ishimi, come out."

The boy hurried to obey. Keiko couldn't tell if there were tears mixed with the water on his face. Funny, he didn't seem frightened. And although she had been terrified in the beginning, now that Shoji was here she felt safe once again. Foolish perhaps, since they were standing in the middle of an Arizona thunderstorm.

Bolts of lightning continued to light up the darkening landscape. It amazed Keiko that it had grown so dark so quickly.

Shoji took her by the hand, grabbing Ishimi with his other. "We have to hurry."

Keiko tried to keep up with Shoji's long footsteps. For every one of his, she had to take three. What must it be like for little Ishimi? Shoji finally seemed to realize the situation. He hoisted the boy into his arms and continued striding along.

Before long they reached barracks fifty-four. Keiko didn't think she knew anyone here, but she knew they would be taken in.

The first door he knocked on brought a response for Shoji. The elderly man who answered his knock stared in surprise before quickly ushering them inside.

His wife hovered around them, her hands flailing helplessly about her. She reminded Keiko of a little hen, her clucking somehow soothing. Ishimi clung to Keiko's wet skirt, his almond eyes wide with the uncertainty of the situation.

They declined the couple's offer of dry clothes, knowing that the storm was already beginning to subside. The rumbles of thunder became farther and farther apart until they were an echo in the distance.

Thanking the couple for their hospitality, Shoji picked the now exhausted Ishimi up in his arms. He followed Keiko to the barracks where he knew the little boy's mother would be frantic with worry.

"Did your mother know where you were going?" he asked Ishimi.

When the boy ducked his head without answering, Shoji had his answer.

"You should never leave without telling your mother where you are going. Never! Do you hear me?"

Ishimi's small voice returned to him from the depths of his shirt front. "Yes, Shoji. I won't do it again."

"You better not, because if I find out you do, I will personally spank your backside."

Even in the dark Keiko could read his look. He meant the same for her, and she had no doubt that he would do just that. It had been childish of her to go so far in her fit of pique.

Ishimi's small voice brought Shoji's head closer to the little boy. "I lost my fish," he sniffed.

Keiko caught her breath at the tender look Shoji bestowed on the small child. His eyes were filled with a warmth she had rarely seen. He would make such a wonderful father.

"We will get you some more. You and I together. Hai?"

Eyes sparkling with delight, Ishimi nodded his head.

Moments later Shoji handed Ishimi over to his grateful mother. Her worried tears brought forth a response from her now repentant son. Keiko was fairly certain the boy would never wander off by himself again.

When they got back to their own apartment, they had to

slush their way through the mud to their small porch. Keiko was thankful that Shoji had built the small structure now. At least they could remove their shoes before going into their apartment.

They both stripped their sodden clothes from their bodies. Standing in her slip, Keiko was shivering from reaction and cold. How could it be 110 degrees one minute and nearly freezing the next? California was nothing like this.

When Keiko turned to pick up her dry shirt, she found Shoji watching her. Butterflies started tumbling about in her stomach and she couldn't take her eyes from his.

When he walked across the small space and took her shirt from her lifeless fingers, Keiko did nothing to protest. He wrapped his arms about her, pulling her into his warm embrace. Sliding her hands up his bare arms, she willed him to continue.

His eyes darkened in response and Keiko knew with a certainty that the time of her waiting had come to an end. Inevitably, his lips found hers and Keiko sighed with pleasure. She gave herself up willingly to the fiery pleasure surrounding her.

The heat from their passion soon had Keiko warm all over. For the time being, she could forget Shoji's still sodden jeans that pressed against her. Nothing mattered to her at this moment except the pleasure she felt in her husband's embrace. She had missed their shared passion, for it was at these times that she felt most loved.

When she heard a soft pounding, it seemed to come from far away. At first she thought it must be the thundering of Shoji's heart so close to her face. When Shoji pulled reluctantly away from her, she realized it was not.

"The door," he told her wryly, and Keiko became aware that the sound she had heard was someone's thunderous knocking against their apartment.

Keiko watched Shoji disappear around the blanket and heard him open the door. An agitated voice drifted clearly back to her from the opening.

"Shoji-san, you come! Tochigi-san, he in hospital. Heart. Not good. Not good. You come."

twelve

Benko set a cup of tea in front of Keiko, but Keiko wasn't aware of it. Papa-san was gone. Dead. Her mind refused to acknowledge the fact. What would she ever do without Papa-san?

Throwing her head on her arms, Keiko let the grief wash over her in waves. She hadn't felt such agony since her mother had passed from this life.

The tears refused to come. It was as though she were made of ice, as though every part of her were frozen and would never thaw again.

She ached to have Shoji take her in his arms and soothe away the pain. She wanted him to be with her, but she knew he was making arrangements about the burial of her father.

Time passed slowly. Nighttime turned to dawn and then into a full-fledged day. Still Shoji didn't come.

At one point in time Keiko slept. When she awakened she was more tired than if she had not slept at all. Her dreams had been sweet, she knew that, but she couldn't remember them.

"Keiko-san," Benko pled, "please lay down on the cot. You can use mine."

Keiko lifted sorrow-filled eyes and stared at her blankly. The effort to move proved to be too much for Keiko. Shaking her head, she lay it back down on her crossed arms.

"I'm okay, Obāsan. I will be fine."

Benko frowned at the lifeless voice, but she kept her own counsel. What Keiko needed most right now was the healing hand of time.

❧

It was after two o'clock in the afternoon before Shoji knocked

146

on the door. When Benko let him in, his eyebrows rose in question.

Benko shook her head, motioning to Keiko's form bent over the table. Shoji went to her, his hands gently massaging her shoulders.

"Keiko, it is time to go home now."

Her tired voice drifted back over her shoulder. "Someone needs to tell Kenji."

Shoji's eyes found Benko's. A look of understanding passed between them.

"I will come stay with her tomorrow," Benko told Shoji softly, and he nodded in agreement.

Shoji bent to his haunches beside Keiko. "I have already sent word to Kenji."

Keiko turned lackluster eyes to his face. "Thank you."

Shoji studied her weary face a moment before rising to his feet. Reaching down, he lifted Keiko into his arms. Instead of protesting, she hung limply against his chest, burrowing her head in his shoulder. Benko held the door open for him, patting his shoulder sympathetically as he passed her.

When they reached the apartment, Shoji placed Keiko on one of the cots, pulling a sheet over her even though it was past a hundred degrees. He had felt her shivering against him and knew she was suffering from shock.

Keiko lay quietly while Shoji moved about the apartment doing things that needed to be done. He worried that her mind refused to focus on anything except Papa-san.

Although Tochigi-san had continued to have Keiko read from her mother's Bible in the evenings, and although he often attended the Christian church here in camp, still he had never made it known to her whether he accepted Christ as his savior. Now, it was too late. Shoji knew that she suffered from the guilt of not knowing. . .not making sure.

Keiko slept so soundly that she didn't stir at Benko arriving and Shoji leaving. Nor did she waken when Shoji returned two hours later. It was as though she were sleeping the sleep of the dead.

Shoji fixed a can of soup and sat eating it alone, watching and worrying about his wife. He was even more worried about what would happen when she found out that Kenji had gone to France and was now missing in action.

Sighing, he leaned his tired face into his palms. Where was it all going to end? Keiko was already on the verge of snapping. What would happen if she lost Kenji, too?

Pushing his half-empty bowl aside, Shoji went and hunkered down next to Keiko's cot. He brushed the tendrils of damp hair from her cheeks, placing his lips where his fingers had been.

She looked so angelic laying there. Dark lashes fanned across light brown skin that had deepened in color due to the Arizona sun. Her lips worked softly in her sleep, almost like a baby's.

His own eyes darkened with tenderness. He would be less than alive if anything happened to her, and he knew it. She had woven her way into his heart so tightly that it would be impossible to remove her. Did she feel the same about him? She responded to his kisses in a most gratifying manner, but that was not love. Or was it? Surely a girl like Keiko would not share such passion with a man she had no feelings for.

Kissing her again, he returned to his now-cold lunch. Closing his eyes, he began to pray.

❧

For the next two days Shoji watched Keiko move as though in a dream. She had understood that they would be unable to attend her father's funeral because Shoji had arranged for the body to be sent back to California to be laid to rest next to her mother. It angered her that she couldn't go, but she said she was thankful that her father wouldn't be buried in the pauper's cemetery in Phoenix.

Shoji saw her responses improve, but still worried. So at

last he told her about his purchase of her father's farm. He could not bear to see her without hope for the future, even if it meant he would never know if she would love him without obligation.

When Keiko questioned Shoji about his keeping the information from her, he gave her a noncommittal answer.

That day, Shoji's mother arrived again. He was grateful for her compassion and sympathy for Keiko and he was relieved to find Keiko sobbing into his mother's arms after two days of stoically enduring her grief. But he ached to be the one to comfort her. Ever at a loss before tears, Shoji left the apartment and wandered through the camp.

Already many barracks were losing people. Some Japanese had been allowed to return to Japan as had been their desire. Many others had found sponsors and jobs outside the encampments and had moved away—some as far away as New York, Chicago, and parts of Florida. "Repatriation," they called it. Shoji snorted. Imagine repatriating American citizens.

When Shoji returned to the apartment, Keiko and his mother were sitting at the table having the inevitable cup of tea. He pulled a cup from the storage cabinet and poured himself a cup of the brew before turning to his mother.

"How did you get here so quickly, Mother? Fly?"

She nodded her head. "I came as soon as I got your telegram."

Shoji barely heard her. He was studying Keiko's face, sighing with relief when he noticed that some of the color had returned to her features. Although the eyes she turned his way were still filled with pain, they now glowed with fresh life. It had been good for his mother to come. Keiko missed a woman's presence in her life, that was probably why she loved Benko so much.

"Sit down, David, I have something to discuss with you."

Shoji frowned at his mother. He would rather not discuss things in front of Keiko right now, not until he was sure she could handle it.

Ignoring his look, Mrs. Ibaragi turned to Keiko. "I told David several months ago that I could get you and him out of this camp. He refused because I couldn't arrange things for your father. Now, however, things are a little different."

Flinching at his mother's lack of couth, Shoji went to stand beside Keiko. His hand rested protectively on her shoulder.

When Mrs. Ibaragi fixed her eyes on her son, they were dark with some unnamed emotion. "David, I can no longer get you out of here."

Shoji sat down in surprise. "Why? If anything, I would think it was easier."

"Not since you answered no to question twenty-seven."

Shoji hadn't realized he was so tense until he felt himself relax. Pressing his lips together, he sighed heavily.

"I see."

"I'm still working on it, but so far I haven't had any luck. Your grandfather is less than pleased."

Shoji leaped to his feet and began pacing the floor. "My grandfather be hanged!"

Both Keiko and Mrs. Ibaragi stared at him in surprise, their mouths hanging open.

Snapping her lips together, Mrs. Ibaragi rose to her feet, fixing her son with a steely glare. "I have arranged to stay with one of the Anglo schoolteachers here. I don't wish to inconvenience you, and I know Keiko doesn't need the added burden right now." She began gathering her things together. "I'll see you some time tomorrow."

Filled with remorse, Shoji met her at the door. His anger at his grandfather had reflected itself upon his mother for years now. Why had she allowed his father to send him away when they had been such a close family? Knowing his mother, she could have done something to prevent it. But she hadn't. Studying her face, he suddenly realized how old she looked. She was still a beautiful woman, but hidden beneath her carefully applied makeup, time was creeping up on her.

"I'm sorry, Mother."

Unexpectedly, she smiled at him. "I know, Son. It's not easy being the grandson of Andrew McConnell. Trust me, I understand. If you think being his grandson is tough, you should try being his daughter."

After she left, Keiko raised questioning eyes to her husband. "Andrew McConnell, of McConnell Aeronautics?"

He rubbed his neck tiredly before turning to her. His eyes were an unfathomable dark brown.

"The same."

Keiko nodded in understanding. "That makes a lot of things clear."

Shoji refused to talk about it, but Keiko continued as though he had encouraged her to.

"I remember hearing about Andrew McConnell's daughter giving up her wealth and going to Japan to be a missionary. Her father disinherited her."

Shoji snorted. "Until he realized he wouldn't have any other children. And it wasn't because she went to Japan to be a missionary that he disowned her. It was because she married a Japanese."

"I'm sorry."

"Why? What do you have to be sorry for? Since I was the only child that would ever be a grandchild of his, he decided to acknowledge his daughter after all. But he never did my father."

"You sound as though you hate him."

Leaning his palms against the storage bureau, Shoji glared up at the ceiling.

"I don't hate him. At least I don't think I do. I just resent his always trying to run my mother's and my life." His face twisted with anger when he turned to her. "I want nothing to do with him. I just want him to leave me alone. That's why I wouldn't accept my mother's offer to get us out of here."

He looked at her apologetically. "And because I knew we

couldn't leave Papa-san."

Keiko sighed heavily, rising and taking the cups to the basin of water she kept in the corner.

"What now?" she asked him.

He sat back down in his seat. "I don't know. We'll have to wait and see."

She picked up her knitting from a chair in the corner that his mother had brought with her on one of her earlier visits. The overstuffed armchair seemed to fit right into its new home. Keiko sat down and began to knit furiously. Shoji had no idea if she knew what she was doing, or whether she would have to take everything out and start again.

"What about Kenji?"

Shoji's eyes flew to her down-bent head. Was she suspicious, or had someone already told her that he was missing?

"What about him?"

She looked at him in surprise. "Will he be able to go to Papa-san's funeral?"

Taking a deep breath, Shoji bit his bottom lip. He had to tell her something. "Keiko, Kenji has been sent overseas. France, I think."

She dropped the knitting, her hands visibly shaking. "Then there's no way he can have gotten the message yet."

Shoji avoided her eyes. "Probably not."

"Poor Sumiko."

When she rose from the chair, Shoji followed her with his eyes. "What are you going to do?"

She began pulling paper from the bureau drawer. "I'm going to write Sumiko."

Deciding that it couldn't hurt, Shoji said nothing. By the time Sumiko could answer, he would have told Keiko the truth about Kenji anyway.

That night they lay in separate bunks thinking separate thoughts. Shoji had dealt with his own grief in his own way. He had no idea how to help Keiko. Surely it affected women differently than men. He was unaware of his *kibei* training in such thoughts.

Keiko slept fitfully, her dreams not so pleasant this time. She was trying to find Kenji, only he was surrounded by fire. Every time she thought she would reach him, flames would leap into her way. She knew she was his only hope of survival, but she couldn't get to him.

Whenever she thought she was about to reach him, Shoji would appear, pulling her inexorably away from her brother. His smiling face did nothing to dispel her fears.

Suddenly, the whole scene burst into flames and Kenji was swallowed up by the conflagration. Screaming, she tried to fight her way to his side, but Shoji held her back. She fought against his iron grip, but she couldn't free herself. She screamed. "Kenji! No!"

A slap across the face brought Keiko fully awake. Tears were streaming down her face and she stared at her husband uncomprehendingly.

He looked as shaken as she felt. "I'm sorry," he told her apologetically, his voice hoarse with emotion. "I couldn't get you to wake up."

Her glazed look roamed across Shoji's face and she began to moan. "You wouldn't let me save him!" Rolling her head from side to side, she tried to push Shoji's hands from her shoulder. "You wouldn't let me save Kenji."

A chill raced down Shoji's spine at her words. Had he somehow been responsible for this nightmare? Had Keiko discerned the situation with Kenji even though he had said nothing?

"It's just a dream, Keiko," he crooned. "Just a dream."

Her level gaze held his. "What's happened to Kenji?"

Shoji rose slowly to his feet, his eyes going everywhere but near Keiko. She gripped his arm with her fingers.

"Shoji?"

He fought with himself several minutes before he finally

breathed out harshly, focusing his gaze on his wife. She had risen on one elbow, reclining against the bed. He carefully sat down next to her.

Taking her hands in his, he told her what she wanted to know. She took the news calmly and Shoji felt relief. She didn't say much, laying back against the cot.

"I'm sorry I didn't tell you," he told her softly.

"This time I understand."

They exchanged a long look that left Keiko feeling as though the sun were surely about to rise. Since it was only a little past three in the morning, she had to smile at her own foolish thinking.

"Get some sleep," Shoji commanded quietly.

Nodding, Keiko watched as he went back to his own cot. She turned her look to the window above her bed. The stars were shimmering brightly against the dark Arizona sky. Somewhere, those same stars were shining down on her brother. Closing her eyes, she began to pray. Her last waking thought was of her brother, but she no longer feared for him. Somehow she knew God was watching out for him. She felt the peace of God enter her soul and wash away all her anxieties.

❧

Shoji stared at the slip of paper in his hands. A buddy of Kenji's had decided to write to let them know more about Kenji's disappearance.

Shoji felt a thrill of pride that his brother-in-law was a member of the famed 442nd. Entirely Japanese, they were fast becoming the most decorated unit in the whole United States Army.

While their unit was fighting a severe battle on the outskirts of Italy, Kenji had somehow become separated from them. One soldier had found Kenji's canteen on the banks of a small river, but there was no other sign of him. It was believed that Kenji must have been wounded and possibly slipped into the river. Since it flowed behind enemy lines, there was no way they could follow its course to find out if their theory was correct.

It was just possible, the soldier's letter went on, that Kenji would be picked up by the French or Italian underground. Shoji prayed that would be the case.

Crumpling the paper in his hand, Shoji stared out the window at the surrounding desert. He would have to tell Keiko. He had promised. But he sure didn't relish the idea. All he wanted was to spare her more pain than she had already endured.

He glared at the sky overhead. *How long, God? How much more can she take?*

Immediately, he was filled with a sense of shame. What a foolish assumption to believe he knew more about Keiko than the One who had created her. How arrogant.

Closing his eyes, he whispered a prayer for Keiko and another one for Kenji. His pride in both knew no bounds. They had become the family he had craved for years now. Even Papa-san.

Shoji felt renewed pain at their loss. He couldn't have loved Keiko's father more if the old man had been his own father. No wonder the two men had been such good friends. They were much alike.

Closing the post office door behind him, he quickly made his way across the compound.

thirteen

Keiko stared at the wall calendar. December seventh. Had it already been two years since that fateful day when the Japanese had sent their bombers to Pearl Harbor and changed Keiko's world forever? In many ways it seemed much longer.

Shortly after the news of Kenji's disappearance, Sumiko had gone into labor. Keiko fretted until word came that Sumiko had delivered a healthy baby girl. With the arrival of her daughter, Sumiko had something positive to occupy her thoughts and time.

Pulling herself from her reflections, Keiko lifted her coat from the chair and slid her arms into the sleeves. She would have to hurry if she wanted to make it to the barracks that housed the Christian church before noon.

As Keiko walked along, she noticed many of the older *issei* working on their barrack homes even though the temperatures were barely above freezing. Whoever heard of freezing temperatures in a desert?

Many people were stuffing newspapers in the half-inch cracks between the wall boards, trying to help keep the cold winds from penetrating to the less than warm interiors.

Some of the barracks boasted Christmas wreaths on their doors, but there were very few. The main religion in this camp was Buddhist, although there were still quite a few Christians.

Keiko smiled at the tumbleweed snowman sitting at the corner of the church barracks. Someone had taken the time to spray paint it white, adding bits of vegetables for the eyes and nose. The resourcefulness of the Japanese people continually amazed her. There was very little thrown away, and what was trash to one was something needed to another. Everything that might have been discarded seemed to have been reused and made into something useful.

Even Shoji had used pieces of leftover pipe and cord to create a wind chime that was the envy of everyone in their block. Of course, Shoji being Shoji, he then set about making one for each family who requested one.

Keiko entered the building, thankful for the stove that warmed it to at least tolerable temperatures. Unbuttoning her jacket, she searched the building for the minister, Mr. Takai. No one else seemed to be around, so she began pulling out decorations for the play the children were to perform on Christmas Eve.

Before long she heard sounds from outside, laughter mingled with excited chatter. Children began filing into the room, their bright eyes sparkling with the joy of the season.

Ishimi ran across the room, flinging himself to his knees beside Keiko.

"Hi, Keiko."

She returned his smile. "Hello, Ishimi. Are you ready to practice?"

He solemnly nodded his head, and Keiko hid a smile at Ishimi's seriousness over the part of playing Joseph, the father of Jesus.

Mr. Takai followed the children into the room, taking off his glasses, which had frosted over. His short, rotund body made Keiko think of him as a sort of Japanese Santa Claus. When he donned a white beard for the occasion, his transformation would be complete.

He grinned at Keiko. "Hello, Keiko. Will Shoji be coming later?"

"Yes, Mr. Takai. He has to work until two o'clock and then he will come help with the scenery."

The minister nodded his head absently as he flipped through the sheets of dialogue in his hands. Today would be spent practicing scenes because the parts had been decided long ago.

Rounding up the chattering children, Keiko had them practice taking their positions on the small stage that Shoji had built just for the occasion.

For weeks now Keiko had been helping the minister with his Christmas program. It was something she needed as much as he had need of her, for she found herself without much to do and too much time to think. The children were a joy to her and kept her busy making costumes, practicing scenes, making scenery. And once again she felt useful, a feeling that had been lacking since Papa-san had died.

She found Ishimi's eyes going to the door as often as Keiko's. The boy's feeling for Shoji had developed into a hero worship that caused Keiko's lips to twitch with amusement. He had lately become Shoji's shadow. Shoji didn't seem to mind, in fact he somewhat encouraged it, knowing that Ishimi had no father figure in his life except an uncle who was a devout Buddhist.

Keiko had studied with Iku Sawada, Ishimi's mother, and she had accepted Christ months ago. Now Iku struggled with her family's obvious disapproval. It would be a battle for her, that much was for sure, but Iku was a very determined young woman. It was sad that she was a widow so young and with a small child to care for without his father's influence.

Shoji and Keiko tried to help her in any way they could, but the biggest help seemed to come from the boy's devotion to Shoji. Keiko felt a tightness in her chest as she thought again about what a good father Shoji would make.

The door opened and Mrs. Tsushima blew in with the wind. It was the only way to describe Mrs. Tsushima. She was young, not much older than Keiko, yet she had experienced more in her life than Keiko imagined she would probably ever experience in hers.

She breezed over to Keiko, her voice preceding her. "Keiko,

I'm so glad you're here. Could you possibly take little Marie for awhile? Honestly, the child is teething and she's an absolute terror about it."

The loving look Mrs. Tsushima bestowed on her baby girl gave lie to her words. She handed the baby to Keiko, gently unwrapping her daughter from the confines of the blankets she had carried her in.

Keiko eagerly took the little girl into her arms, smiling down at Marie's cherubic features. Marie waved chubby brown fists at Keiko, gurgling happily. Her bright almond eyes and dark hair were very similar to those of the woman smiling down at her.

As Keiko played with Marie, she couldn't help but wish for a child of her own. It had become almost an obsession with her. Since the night of her father's death, Shoji had taken great pains to avoid being alone with her. She knew he was again avoiding any chance of conceiving children of their own, and her own heart ached. Not only with the knowledge that she wouldn't have a child of her own any time soon, but also with the pain of separation from the one man she loved most in the world.

Although he was with her in the evenings, he was still distant, forcing her to reconcile herself to the fact that his stubbornness far exceeded her own. The realization that he suffered as much as she did, did nothing to alleviate her own pain.

As usual, thoughts of babies brought Sumiko to mind. Kenji was still missing and hope was growing dim that he would be found alive. After five months, the odds were against it.

Keiko hugged Marie tighter, bringing forth a protesting yelp from the small baby. Would Sumiko wind up like Iku, a young widow with a child that would never know its father? *Dear God, please don't let it be so.*

When Shoji came, the children seemed to settle down and rehearsals went more smoothly. Even the younger girls responded to Shoji's magnetism and tried to outdo each other in a bid for his attention and a word of praise.

Keiko watched him, her heart in her eyes. When his eyes met hers, his were caught and held by the intensity of emotion he witnessed there. Only for a moment did they find themselves in seeming isolation before Ishimi latched onto Shoji's knees and drew his attention away.

Later that evening, when Keiko and Shoji were at the mess hall, Shoji told Keiko that he had arranged for her to visit Sumiko for Christmas.

She began making plans for their trip, but Shoji placed his large hand over her smaller one.

"Not me, Keiko-chan. I could only arrange for you to go."

Keiko's brows puckered into a frown. "I can't go without you. It's Christmas. I can't just leave you here." Her voice began to rise. "I won't do it."

"Shhh. Lower your voice." Shoji's eyes went around the room and came back to her. "I think Sumiko would like to see you. I think she needs to see you."

Keiko struggled with the desire to go and the need to remain. Sumiko had her mother, father, and baby Esther, Shoji had only her. She began shaking her head again.

"If you're worried about me being alone, don't be. My mother is coming to stay for a few weeks."

Somewhat relieved, Keiko still hesitated. This would be little Esther's first Christmas and Keiko would love to be there for that, but still, could she just leave Shoji?

He was finally able to convince her, and Keiko would be eternally grateful for that.

❧

The time she spent with Sumiko was good for both of them. They gained strength from each other, both sure in their knowledge that Kenji would be okay.

Before she left, Keiko studied Esther thoroughly, trying to memorize each little detail as a picture in the memory book of her mind.

Keiko hadn't realized just how much she would miss Shoji, and although part of her longed to remain, nothing could have induced her to stay; so when the bus left Topaz Relocation Center, she was on it.

The day she arrived back at Butte Camp, Shoji met Keiko with the news that Kenji had been found alive. Word had reached Shoji while Keiko was still en route. Kenji would be returning to the states soon. Both Keiko and Shoji went to their knees to thank God for His goodness and to ask His continuing protection over them all.

৯

As the months passed, Keiko found little jobs at the school and at the church to keep her occupied. Shoji still worked at the model ship factory, but he refused to even consider Keiko doing the same.

"I don't want you to work. If you want to help one of the teachers or teach a class on origami or something, that's fine, but I don't want you working."

Although she felt his attitude was a little archaic, still she bowed to his headship of their family. Actually, she was rather pleased, because in truth she had no desire to be anything other than a wife and mother. The problem was, Shoji was gone all day and she couldn't foresee motherhood in the near future the way things were going. Deciding to do the next best thing, Keiko volunteered at the day nursery.

Early in 1944, word came that Butte Camp would be closing by the next year. Since Italy had secretly surrendered in September 1943, hope was high that an end to the war was in sight. Only the battle with Japan and Germany was still being waged, but it seemed that Germany was fast losing steam. Japan was another matter.

Keiko continued to pray because although Kenji had returned home and was still recuperating, if the war continued, he could still be recalled. His letters to her were full of his little girl, and Keiko rejoiced at his fatherly love. She also sympathized with his chafing at the delay in getting them out of camp and into a normal home.

Many of the Japanese were being allowed to leave, but the West Coast was still off-limits. Still, they were finding new homes and new lives in other parts of the country. Mrs. Roosevelt had stated that this was a good brought about by the war, and perhaps it was, but Keiko was still angered by the way in which it was accomplished.

Since no official word had come yet about the center closing, only the rumors that ran rampant among their facility, Shoji maintained his stubbornness in refusing to take a chance on starting a family. Keiko marveled at his self-control. Many times they had come to the brink of forgetting, but Shoji would always pull back.

June arrived with its scorching temperatures. Using his ingenuity, Shoji devised a sort of evaporative cooling system. They could have purchased a real evaporative cooler like some people did, but Shoji felt better using his own devices.

Keiko was thankful for the relief from the oppressive heat when she was in her own apartment. Often she had company, people trying to avoid the hot part of the day. Fans proved almost less than useful, though they were better than nothing.

Shoji came in from work nearly exhausted from the hot temperatures. He lay his head back against the overstuffed chair, rubbing his hands tiredly across his face. Keiko could sense trouble, though Shoji had said nothing.

She brought him a glass of tea that she had been cooling by wrapping it with wet clothes and letting the air from the fan blow on it. It was amazing just how cool this could make things, even in the soaring temperatures.

He thanked her, chugging down the drink without pause.

"Is something wrong?" she asked him, sitting on the arm of the chair.

His eyes met hers as he handed her back the glass. "The

allies invaded Normandy two days ago. Thousands of Americans are dead."

A cold numbness entered her body, raising the flesh on her skin into tiny bumps. *Thousands*, he had said.

He pulled her down onto his lap and she buried her head against his chest. How much longer? How much longer would this insanity go on? How many more people had to die?

He held her a long time before rousing himself to the time. "They'll be serving supper soon."

Keiko shook her head. "I'm not hungry. You go ahead."

"I'm not hungry, either, but I want to see if there's any more news. Sure you don't want to come?"

Deciding that she preferred his company to her own, she went with him. The noise level in the mess hall was louder than usual, making Keiko believe that word was spreading rapidly of recent developments.

Keiko listened in fascination as the men discussed the how's and wherefore's of the invasion of Normandy's coast. Closing her eyes, she could see bodies floating en masse in the waters of the English Channel. Shivering, she got up and fled back to her apartment.

On July 18, the shocking news came that Japan's Prime Minister Tojo had resigned. Ripples of feeling regarding this action spread throughout the camp. Was Japan beginning to crumble?

In that same month an attempt was made on Hitler's life. Perhaps it was un-Christian of her to feel it, but Keiko was sorry that the attempt had failed. She considered the man a monster, and she struggled daily with her own evil thoughts regarding the man.

Fall was fast approaching and Keiko dreaded spending another Christmas in Butte Camp. Last year Mr. Takai had done much to make Christmas at the camp seem homelike and reminded them constantly of the purpose for the season. Still, Keiko wanted to be in her own home, planning her own

Christmas dinner and putting up a tree with lights.

More and more the rumors spread of a possible ending to the war. Keiko began to have hope that her wish might come true.

In October, Keiko received another letter from Sumiko, this time telling her that Kenji was returning to his unit. Keiko felt as though the bottom had dropped out of her world. The one good thing that Sumiko had to tell her was that Sumiko's father had been offered a job in San Antonio, Texas, and that they would be leaving immediately to take it. Sumiko and Esther would be going with them.

Keiko told Shoji when he came home that evening.

"Thank God!" was all he said.

Not many nights later, Shoji came home from work and Keiko could tell he had something on his mind. He took Keiko in his arms, kissing her long and hard.

Surprised, Keiko searched his face for some clue to his mood. Finding none, she leaned back against his arm, a tentative smile forming on her lips.

"Okay, what have you been up to?"

He returned her smile with one of his own. His eyes took on a gleam as they roved over her face. "We're leaving here."

The smile deserted Keiko. "What? When? How?"

Shoji sat down, pulling her down with him. "I've been offered a job in Palm Beach."

Thoroughly confused, Keiko waited for him to continue.

"My grandfather owns the plane manufacturing plant there. He used his influence, pulled some strings, and there you have it."

Confusing emotions skittered around inside Keiko. She was thrilled to be leaving Butte Camp, but the thought of all the friends she would leave behind caused her a pang of loss. What would she ever do without Benko's love and guidance? And Ishimi! What would happen to him without Shoji there to lead the way?

Her eyes found Shoji's. The very inscrutableness of his

look told her more than he would say.

"You don't want to go, do you?"

His feigned look of surprise didn't fool her. He opened his mouth to deny it, but Keiko covered his lips with her hand.

"I know how you feel about your grandfather. I know you don't want to be beholden to him for anything."

His eyes softened. Kissing her fingers, he removed them from his mouth. "I love you more than my pride. I know how badly you want to start a family, and I refuse to consider it under these circumstances. I want a family, too. But more than that, I want to hold you in my arms again like before this whole war came about."

Keiko knew how much it had cost him to lower his pride, and she felt an overwhelming flood of love for him.

"I can't let you do that."

His eyes took on that steely look that she had come to recognize as his desire to have his own way. Placing her lips against his, she hushed him with a kiss.

"Listen to me for a change. This war can't last much longer. You said so yourself. With everything that's happened, surely the end must be in sight. Why else are the rumors growing stronger every day that this camp will be closed soon?" She searched his eyes with her own. "We've waited this long, we can wait a little longer."

He smiled wryly. "I'm not so sure I can."

She blushed at his inference, but her eyes glowed with love. "If nothing changes by the end of this year. . .well, then we'll consider your grandfather's offer."

Shoji sighed heavily. "Two months is an awfully long time."

"So is two years," she admonished him gently.

His eyes twinkled back at her. "You have no idea!"

"Haven't I?"

Swallowing hard, Shoji gently pushed Keiko from his lap. "Okay," he told her, his voice raw with emotion. "But if nothing changes by the end of this year, then I will accept my grandfather's offer."

"Hai," she told him softly. She knew how painful it would be for her husband to submit to someone who so obviously disliked his father. Keiko decided it would be best to pray for a quick end to this war—not that she hadn't been doing so for nearly three years.

On December 17, 1944, official word came down that Butte Camp would close the following year. For the first time in three years there was hope that the end of this war was imminent.

Immediately, families were encouraged to seek employment outside of the camp. Anyone who had a job lined up was given clearance to leave, but the West Coast was still a forbidden zone.

Since Keiko and Shoji's farm was in California, they knew they would have to bide their time, hoping against hope that California would be freed from restriction soon.

The official date for Butte Camp to close was set for November 15, 1945, over eleven months away. Since the war with Germany and Japan was still being waged, this seemed a premature presumption that the United States would win. Still, the euphoric feelings were running high.

For many of the *issei* and *kibei*, this was a sad time. The death toll on both sides was high, and many of the Japanese wondered about their families still in Japan. Shoji was one of them. There was no way to get word to or from family and friends.

With the beginnings of closure of the camp, Shoji and Keiko decided to stay and help their friends with their relocation. Shoji helped Benko and her family load their goods onto a truck, while Keiko cried in the older woman's arms.

"I will miss you, Obāsan," Keiko told her.

"And I you. But someday we will meet again. You taught me this."

Keiko realized that Benko was referring to her recent conversion to Christianity. She and Keiko had studied for months together, and Benko had decided that the Christian religion "made sense," as she put it.

"I hope we don't have to wait for heaven, Obāsan," Keiko told her. The old woman merely smiled before climbing into the army truck.

Keiko listlessly prepared a meal for Shoji and herself since they had missed the five o'clock meal. Her heart was heavy for the loss of her friends, but she was thankful that they were finally resuming a normal life.

When Keiko pushed through the curtain that separated their sleeping quarters from their living quarters, she stopped dead in surprise. There, sitting in the middle of the room, was a double bed with mattress and box springs.

Shoji put his arms around her from behind, nuzzling his lips against her neck. She turned her head slightly, her eyes full of questions.

"Benko's son said he didn't need it. I bought it from him."

She turned in his arms, a happy glow filling her eyes. Drawing his lips down to hers, Keiko told him without words just how happy he had made her. Shoji lifted her in his arms and carried her to the bed.

epilogue

March 1946

Keiko lifted the doll from the box beside her, smiling at the gift from Shoji. Her very own Bodhidharma doll stared sightlessly back at her.

Picking up the small paintbrush sitting on the table beside her, Keiko carefully colored in one tiny eye. Smiling, she set the doll on the shelf to dry.

She reached into the bassinet beside her, stroking the soft, dark hair on her son's tiny head. "I will fill in the other eye when you accept Christ as your savior," she told him softly. His sleep was undisturbed and Keiko continued to watch him, finding it hard to get her fill of just looking at the little wonder that was part of both Shoji and herself. What a tiny miracle!

The back door slammed open and Keiko had a sense of déjà vu. Lifting her eyes, she almost expected to see Kenji enter the room. Instead, her husband peeked his head around the corner.

Shoji came fully into the room, eyeing the dolls on the shelves much like the first time he had visited this house. He smiled at the new Bodhidharma doll he had ordered for Keiko from Japan and gently stroked the cheek of his son. It was hard to believe that the war was over and trade with Japan continued as though never having been interrupted.

Many years had passed. Some of them good, some of them not so good. For Shoji, there was a feeling of coming home. His anger, his feelings of nonentity, had finally been put to rest with the birth of his son. He now knew just where he belonged, where God had intended him to be from the beginning. He was Keiko's, and she was his, and wherever they were together was home.

In April 1945 Hitler had committed suicide, and seven days later Germany had surrendered. For all intents and purposes the war had ended. Only Japan had refused to give in.

Even an atomic bomb dropped on Hiroshima in August hadn't budged them. It was only after a second one was dropped on Nagasaki that they had finally sued for peace in September. Had it really only been six months ago?

Shoji knelt beside his wife and son. His eyes were tender when they finally connected with Keiko's.

"I see you've colored in your first eye."

"Hai," she answered softly, bending forward and swiftly kissing his lips. "Now I will begin to pray for the fulfillment of my endeavor."

Shoji watched as Keiko lifted her mother's Bodhidharma doll from its box. The one eye stared grotesquely back at her, much like the new one.

Lifting the paintbrush again, Keiko carefully colored in the other eye of her mother's doll. Her own eyes were filled with tears as she set the doll on the shelf next to the new one.

"I never thought I would be thankful for a war," she told Shoji. "But if not for this war, I'm not sure my brother would ever have accepted Christ."

Shoji reached for Keiko's chin, turning her face toward him. "Only God knows."

Keiko realized that that was true. And only God knew how all of this would end. Someday, maybe this country would finally grant citizenship to the *issei* who had remained faithful and loyal to a country that had betrayed them.

For now, life went on much as it had before the war. She had the farm, but instead of Papa-san, she had Shoji. Instead of Kenji, she had her son, Andrew Shinichi Ibaragi.

Shoji had asked her why she wanted to name him Andrew.

Keiko realized that Shoji wanted his son to have a Japanese heritage as well as an American one, except instead of forcing it on him like his own father had, Shoji hoped to teach his son by example.

She told him that Andrew was her favorite apostle because in every instance recorded in the Bible where Andrew was mentioned, he was bringing someone to Christ. Keiko hoped that her own son would do the same someday. And she chose the name Shinichi after her own father.

Shoji rose to his feet, pulling Keiko up beside him. Placing an arm around her waist, he led her outside to the porch. Together they watched the sun begin its descent below the horizon. Already the fields were ripe with the harvest.

On a hill in the distance, the shadow of two tombstones could be clearly seen against the flaming sky. Keiko hoped that her father was with her mother. She would never know until that day when she would join them, but until then, life went on.

Shoji smiled at her, and Keiko felt for the first time in her life like she really belonged. This was where she wanted to be. Now and forever.

A Letter To Our Readers

Dear Reader:

In order that we might better contribute to your reading enjoyment, we would appreciate your taking a few minutes to respond to the following questions. When completed, please return to the following:

Rebecca Germany, Managing Editor
Heartsong Presents
P.O. Box 719
Uhrichsville, Ohio 44683

1. Did you enjoy reading *The Rising Son?*
   ❑ Very much. I would like to see more books
      by this author!
   ❑ Moderately
      I would have enjoyed it more if _____
      _____

2. Are you a member of **Heartsong Presents**? ❑Yes ❑No
   If no, where did you purchase this book?_____
   _____

3. What influenced your decision to purchase this
   book? (Check those that apply.)

   ❑ Cover   ❑ Back cover copy

   ❑ Title   ❑ Friends

   ❑ Publicity   ❑ Other_____

4. How would you rate, on a scale from 1 (poor) to 5
   (superior), the cover design?_____

5. On a scale from 1 (poor) to 10 (superior), please rate the following elements.

___Heroine   ___Plot

___Hero   ___Inspirational theme

___Setting   ___Secondary characters

6. What settings would you like to see covered in **Heartsong Presents** books?_____

_____

_____

7. What are some inspirational themes you would like to see treated in future books?_____

_____

_____

8. Would you be interested in reading other **Heartsong Presents** titles? ☐ Yes   ☐ No

9. Please check your age range:
   ☐ Under 18   ☐ 18-24   ☐ 25-34
   ☐ 35-45   ☐ 46-55   ☐ Over 55

10. How many hours per week do you read? _____

Name _____

Occupation _____

Address _____

City_____ State_____ Zip _____

Colleen L. Reece takes girls ages 9 to 15 on nail-biting adventures in the Nancy Drew style, but with a clear Christian message. Super sleuth Juli Scott and her savvy friends find love and excitement and learn that it always pays to have a sense of humor. The first two titles in this mystery series are not to be missed.

___***Mysterious Monday***—Julie refuses to believe her father was killed in the line of duty as a policeman. With the help of her new friend Shannon, Julie sets out to reopen the case.

___***Trouble on Tuesday***—Shannon has gotten caught up in fortune telling and an uncanny prediction. In spite of everything her friends try to do, only God can save her from this web of deception.

·····Heart♥ng·····

HEARTSONG PRESENTS TITLES AVAILABLE NOW:

(If ordering from this page, please remember to include it with the order form.)

······· Presents ·······

Great Inspirational Romance at a Great Price!

Heartsong Presents books are inspirational romances in contemporary and historical settings, designed to give you an enjoyable, spirit-lifting reading experience. You can choose wonderfully written titles from some of today's best authors like Peggy Darty, Sally Laity, Tracie J. Peterson, Colleen L. Reece, Lauraine Snelling, and many others.

When ordering quantities less than twelve, above titles are $2.95 each.
Not all titles may be available at time of order.

Hearts♥ng Presents
Love Stories Are Rated G!

That's for godly, gratifying, and of course, great! If you lov
a thrilling love story, but don't appreciate the sordidness of som
popular paperback romances, **Heartsong Presents** is for you. I
fact, **Heartsong Presents** is the *only inspirational romance boo
club*, the only one featuring love stories where Christian faith i
the primary ingredient in a marriage relationship.

Sign up today to receive your first set of four, never befor
published Christian romances. Send no money now; you wil
receive a bill with the first shipment. You may cancel at any tim
without obligation, and if you aren't completely satisfied wit
any selection, you may return the books for an immediate refund

Imagine. . .four new romances every four weeks—two histori
cal, two contemporary—with men and women like you who lon,
to meet the one God has chosen as the love of their lives. . .all fo
the low price of $9.97 postpaid.

*To join, simply complete the coupon below and mail to th
address provided.* **Heartsong Presents** romances are rated G fo
another reason: They'll arrive *Godspeed!*

YES! Sign me up for Hearts♥ng!

NEW MEMBERSHIPS WILL BE SHIPPED IMMEDIATELY!
Send no money now. We'll bill you only $9.97 post-paid with your first
shipment of four books. Or for faster action, call toll free 1-800-847-8270.

NAME _____

ADDRESS _____

CITY _____ STATE _____ ZIP _____

MAIL TO: HEARTSONG PRESENTS, P.O. Box 719, Uhrichsville, Ohio 44683

YES10-96